DESTINY

A Lesson in Building a Stable

Amity Harris

Copyright © 2024 All rights reserved

The characters and events portrayed in this book are fictitious. Any similarity to real persons, living or dead, is coincidental and not intended by the author. The author in no way represents the companies, corporations or brands mentioned in this book. The likeness of historical/famous figures have been used fictitiously; the author does not speak for or represent these people. All opinions expressed in this book are the author's, or are fictional.

No part of this book may be reproduced, or stored in a retrieval system, or transmitted in any form or by any means, electronic, mechanical, photocopying, recording, or otherwise, without express written permission of the author and publisher.

ISBN: 9798323184415

Cover design and publishing by GetMeOnline.today

Dedication

To My Cop. Because he is — and always will be — My Cop.

Contents

Dedication i
Contents iii
Preface v
A Note from Amity vii
Parlor Guests 1
    Chapter 1 1
    Chapter 2 7
    Chapter 3 11
    Chapter 4 19
Slave Contracts 23
    Chapter 5 23
    Chapter 6 35
Remotes and Applicants 39
    Chapter 7 39
    Chapter 8 43
    Chapter 9 49
    Chapter 10 55
Remote Slaves 61
    Chapter 11 61
    Chapter 12 67
Dinner 73
    Chapter 13 73
    Chapter 14 77
    Chapter 15 83
Two Months Ago 85
    Chapter 16 85
    Chapter 16 89
    Chapter 17 95
    Chapter 18 99
Danica's Visit 105

Chapter 19	105
Chapter 20	111
Chapter 21	119
Chapter 22	125
Chapter 23	131
Dinner and Dessert	141
Chapter 24	141
Chapter 25	145
Epilogue	149
Chapter 26	153
Chapter 27	157
Chapter 28	165
Chapter 29	169
Disclaimer	171
About Amity Harris	173
Books by Amity Harris	175

Preface

THE LOCATION WAS PERFECT. Acres of property two hours from anything resembling a city afforded the property owner total seclusion. With a generous gift from the tech executive whose obsession to be a slave she let him live out in real life, she had the land and the funds to create her own heaven. Right here. In Montana.

He had been a useful submissive to her for years. His sudden wealth made his passion to be her slave grow even more. Now he could give her a lot more than just himself. What made it even better was his utter obsession to make her happy. When she was in a good mood, his servitude filled him with joy, the kind of joy he couldn't find anywhere else. Not in the boardroom or with the businesses or properties he owned. His pleasure was inextricably intertwined with her whims.

Building her fantasy filled his days. And his nights.

When he woke up that morning a year ago, alone in the cell she kept him locked and chained, he finally knew how ecstasy felt. That was the morning he decided to satisfy her. No, more than satisfy her. She unlocked him like a can opener on a stubborn can of tuna and he exploded in bliss. What good was his new-found money if she wasn't happy every day?

A few meetings with his attorneys and financial people was all it took to put together the supreme gift he could give her. She already owned his body and mind. Now she could be the Mistress of the land, the place she called Destiny, and once the construction was finished, she could own him even more deeply. He'd buy her more slaves. More like him.

Her dream was a stable of slaves. He would make it real.

The sparsely populated space between Fort Peck and the Fort Belknap reservations was ideal. The Missouri River formed a natural southern border and there was a national park on the east. Besides, who wanted to be a tourist in that god-forsaken country? Privacy, she said. She wanted privacy. He bought it for her.

He had not become successful by speculating on ventures that *might* flourish. No, he studied plans, interviewed startup founders, investigated their funding and scrutinized competitors before investing even a dollar in a business. Gambling was not in his vocabulary. In his limited spare time, he sought out women who exercised power like she did and in exchange for his gifts and a few weeks of surrender in their dungeons and stables, he gained a firm understanding of how to make Destiny her realm.

Once the entire project was completed, he vowed to thank the women who allowed him to serve them temporarily by enlisting their help in choosing the right mix of male slaves she could choose from. To own. Like she owned him.

The crews worked day and night and the buildings were ready to be stocked with rows and rows of tools and custom furniture. All that was left was to gather the slaves to be the final touch on the project. Men she would own. Her slaves. Her stable.

That morning when he woke up alone, caged and chained to the floor, he knew it was time to close the circle. When she came for him and whipped him until she was ready for breakfast, he would ask permission to speak. When she granted his plea, Destiny was hers.

He was thrilled when she stood outside the bars with a whip in her hand. An hour later, his skin raw as meat, he knelt at her feet while she sipped coffee.

"Ma'am?" he asked.

"Three words," she granted him.

He took a deep breath and blurted out his promise to her.

"Destiny is yours."

She sipped from the porcelain cup and looked past him to the sunshine blazing outside the window.

"And yours," she said. The way she said it was as much a promise as it was a threat.

His heart was ready to burst as was the dripping penis that hung between his legs. That was hers, too.

A Note from Amity

DOMMES ARE NOT MADE. We are born with the mysterious hunger for the kind of power that makes us who we were always meant to be. Sometimes women realize their potential by themselves while others are fortunate enough to own the right slaves who — for the right reasons — help them reach their destinies. This is the story of one of them, a natural-born Domme with the good fortune to have the right submissive at the perfect time.

Danica is a woman with the soul and spirit of a Domme who learned she was one of a select few women who shared that appetite early enough to make her dreams come true. She was invited to one of my Parlors, flying clear across the country, to be among women who shared the same belief in their own power. Her Parlor application piqued my interest with a short reply to my question about her experience.

I asked, "Where are you on your journey?"

Danica wrote, "I am a process."

Within with my network of Domme friends, we insist upon and value honesty. Sometimes honesty can be brutal. Danica's answer told me tomes about her, her journey and her integrity. After the Memphis Auction and suffering through Larisa's baseless inflated opinion of herself, it was a pleasure to meet an unpretentious Domme, no matter where she was on her voyage. There is one quality we demand in the women we let into our circle.

Authenticity.

I wanted to get to know Danica better, even more after meeting her at my Parlor. That full-day program was a trip through taking on and breaking new slaves into your stable. The session was requested by two women who were considering admitting new boys to their stables based on applications. Boys who apply have never been owned so there was no one to check with about their usefulness or obedience. It's a big risk to take on a slave from only an application.

In the Parlor we talked about background checks and which agencies were cost-efficient and accurate, how many years back they researched and which databases they had access to. Once you are sure they are not criminals and have the right kind of histories that led them to apply, you need a plan, a system, to bring them into your stable. Beyond that, you have to recognize the warning signs of potential problems and eliminate them fast. A difficult slave will disrupt your stable.

Our applicants sign contracts. We are taking a big chance on them plus there is the cost of their training. Beyond that, there is our outlay to feed and house them. No one wants to devote those resources to a male who may change his mind after his first punishment session.

That is not how it works. Not in my world.

It's a privilege for a slave to live in Amityworld. Slaves, especially applicants, have to appreciate the gift I give them and they must dedicate their lives to showing me their gratitude. Above all else, they must understand what my ownership is. And what it means.

When Danica visited after the Parlor, I encouraged her to return for a few weeks so I could get to know her and perhaps foster her evolution into the Domme she was born to be. She was more than amenable; in fact, she was overjoyed with the invitation. I always bring a hostess gift when I visit. She brought one that didn't fit into a traditional gift box with a satin bow. Hers was much bigger than that.

He had a slave's heart. It overflowed with devotion to his owner and extended to her friends. An authentic slave.

This is the story of Danica's visits to Amityworld and what she learned. With that knowledge, she could settle into Destiny and put her slave's gifts to the best use. It's the tale of how she learned, through trials and errors and successes, how to be an authentic Domme. She experienced our special way of inducting select women into our network. Oh, there were some challenges for sure. But in the end, we welcomed her with open arms. And a single-tail in our hands.

Her slave? I got to know him as well. Before the Parlor, he spent a month in my stable when Danica thought he was tending to business. The boy was desperate to learn what Destiny needed, beyond land and privacy. I taught him to *feel his* slavery and not simply perform it. Two days after he left, I received a handwritten letter of thanks. And a diamond bracelet. Etched inside, it said, "Ms. Amity."

Parlor Guests

CHAPTER 1

THE YOUNG DOMMES

DANICA'S SLAVE'S PLANE landed on time at a private airport, a two-hour drive from my world. I had a limo meet Danica and the other Parlor guests for the ride to my estate. I invited a small group for this Parlor because what I intended to cover was what the invitees needed to learn hands on. Two arrived via a ride share from the main airport and the other three had private planes at their disposal. Only six Dommes were this Parlor's audience. I invited the six who needed this session the most.

Save for a cobalt blue bow tied around his cock, Danica's slave emerged naked from his own plane.

The women rode in the limo's roomy back seat. The slave was stuffed into the rear. Once the window shades were lowered, they couldn't see the route my driver took. Like all first-time guests, they were given instructions.

No one enters my world through the front door the first time, not even Dommes. All visitors must earn their way in.

The limo came to a stop in my transport garage, a windowless building with a concrete floor. My driver that day was Mason, a remote who confessed his submission to me when he supervised the crew I hired to remodel the Parlor building and several out-buildings on my property. I knew he was desperate to submit. He was also a big dose of eye candy.

Mason pressed the button to close the garage door and invited his six passengers to exit the limo. I had a girl meet them, take their clothes and hand out thin jumpsuits that snap up the front. Mason ignored their shocked reactions to the bizarre instruction to strip. Five mouths hung open. Only Danica was stoic. She was the first to take off her clothes and the others followed. Reluctantly.

I watched their faces while they disrobed. One accepted the instruction. Five complained throughout the process.

That was when I first thought about inviting Danica back to my world for private tutoring.

My girl ushered the six jumpsuit-clad, Keds sneaker-wearing women through the only other door in the garage. The path led them to the Intake building where all new slaves — and all visitors no matter their rank or position in the outside world — begin meriting their admission to my world. Every visitor, from slave to Domme, runs down that path. I call it the slaveway.

The Dommes should have been grateful I let them wear jumpsuits for the run. No male gets that consideration. Slaves run naked. Nudity in front of each other and my cameras erases any status they think sets them apart.

Slightly out of breath, the women arrived at Intake and were sent to the main room and told to sit on exam tables. They grumbled, of course, but they sat where they were told.

My purpose in sending guests through modified Intake is twofold. First, there is a basic health check. Parlors are interactive. Guests use tools on the demo slaves and I want to be sure they can swing a whip. I also make sure they are not wearing any electronics that could interfere with my slaves' perineal chips. Besides, we're only a year or so away from that damned pandemic so screening for coughs or stuffy noses and a cursory physical exam makes sense.

There is a second reason I send all visitors through Intake. No matter who you are or your perceived status in your world, there is only one head of state in Amityworld. That is, of course, me. All invitees must comply with that rule or they get an immediate return trip to the airport. Enforcing that policy begins in Intake.

Both of my objectives happen there.

The women were quite a sight. Full makeup, hair fixed but only a thin layer of translucent gray cotton separating them from the world underscored their role while they were here. They were lucky to be allowed into my world and accepting my rules was not negotiable. To a woman, they were thrilled to tell their friends they were invited. Then, like most of my guests, they'd drop my name. And smirk.

A year after I bought Emma at the Swedish Auction, I had *him* turned into *her* and gave her a new name. She is the doctor who takes care of my stable, the household girls, and on occasion, a visiting Domme who needs medical care. She worked meticulously with the Slave Circus Mistress while she recovered from a brutal attack that set her on a long and difficult recovery. She recuperated physically. At the Memphis Auction, my exclusive, Zayn, helped her reach emotional health. When he was done, all was right in her world and her slave circus was reborn.

Emma knew she was a woman in a man's body and that's probably why her former owner put him up for sale. She didn't have the means, medical or financial, to transform him. The network knows I enjoy creating eunuchs and selling them when I'm done with them, but Emma was the first true transgender I had transformed. It was a good decision. She is happy every day and when I let her into the wardrobe closet and makeup room, she is in heaven.

She asked to speak to me a few weeks ago and after she crawled through the half-door into my office, gushed her thanks.

"Ms. Amity, you make me thrilled to wake up every morning."

One of these days, I might give her a single-syllable name, a reward I grant my girls who earn my trust and are completely loyal to me.

The six women on the exam tables sat quietly while I watched them on my monitors. Emma pranced in with her pink stethoscope around her neck and issued an order they were sure to bristle at. Even though she needed to check their heart rates and blood pressure, she could do that through the thin jumpsuits. That's not how it's done in my world.

"Strip," she said. That was it.

Three reluctantly kicked off their Keds sneakers. Two wore faces of total surprise. The last one, Danica, unsnapped her jumpsuit, let it fall to her feet and stepped out of it and her sneakers at the same time. Then she looked at Emma for the next instruction.

Danica was definitely returning to Amityworld. The other five? That was still up in the air.

Once they were disrobed and shoeless, Emma had them lay on the exam tables and took their blood pressure. She does that first because the stress of being naked in front of others often reaches the upper range on the sphygmomanometer. It's set to beep if the reading is too high for a guest to proceed. Undiagnosed high blood pressure is a silent killer, so I look at it as a community service.

Three women were a little high, two were high normal and only one was smack in the middle on conventional charts. Emma would rerun the test before my girl moved them to the next Intake step. For now, she assessed their breathing and measured their heart rates before telling them to line up along the wall.

This part of Intake reinforces two of my main objectives, health and obedience. It also separates true Dommes from wannabees. Even though a cursory rectal exam has health benefits, it is one of the most outrageous exams these six women could imagine being subjected to. They were wrong, of course, because they don't know me. Yet. They would know me a lot better very soon.

Facing the wall, they pressed their hands on it and took two steps back as Emma instructed. It was a good bet they had no idea what she was going to do. They should have figured it out when she snapped a glove on her hand and squeezed a glob of lubrication on her fingers. My guess was they were too embarrassed to admit they knew where her fingers were going.

I switched monitors to see their faces. Close up. Emma's fingers in their asses didn't interest me. Their reactions did. Faces reveal everything.

The first rectum she examined was Martha's. The background check My Cop provided told me her basic stats, 5'5" of heft with a huge bosom and ample layers of fat. I watched her breasts bounce when she jogged down the slaveway to Intake. Her eyes were black and so was her short hair style. The color matched the full bush that covered her lower lips.

Martha knew money. She was a CPA but had no concept of how a rectal exam would make her feel until Emma's fingers slid into her.

"Oh my god," she wailed. "What are you doing?"

Emma doesn't chat with her patients. She doesn't know or care who they are or who they think they are. Slaves and Domme guests are simply bodies for her to evaluate because that is her job.

Emma changed gloves to explore Beatrix's rectum. Beatrix lived near Colorado Springs her whole life, My Cop reported. At 5'6" with an athlete's body, Beatrix's medium-length hair was blonde, probably dyed, and her green eyes were staring blankly at the wall. She was one of the few Dommes who did paid work. A girl's got to pay the bills, she wrote on her Parlor application.

When Emma's slippery fingers slid into her, Beatrix gasped and muttered, "Goddamnit!" She repeated it several times before Emma changed gloves and moved to the next rectum in line.

That one belonged to Parker, a Gulf-coast Florida Domme whose 5'8" height was highlighted by what had to be a 12-month tan. Swimming and surfing gave her a decent body but the interesting fact was the mansion she inherited from her parents. My research said she wanted to convert it into a rental boutique where clients could pay to use her slaves in privacy. That's why she applied for this Parlor, to learn how to grow her stable with quality slaves who could satisfy her clients' kinks in her own facility. It was a worthy goal. A lucrative one, too. I leaned closer to my monitor when Emma's fingers found her ass.

When two of Emma's fingers slipped in, I heard it clear as day.

"Ooh, ooh," she cooed and spread her feet farther apart.

It's not every Domme who relishes fingers in her ass. I would have to take a closer look at Parker. She might have promise.

Simone, a Cocoa Beach Domme, lived on Florida's Atlantic coast. She was tall, standing at 5'8" with a massive pair of breasts and a career in business. Like Parker, she had a Florida tan but unlike Parker, she carried an arrogant attitude. That would have to go. No one bosses my slaves around except me. I was curious how she would interact with Emma.

Glove, lube, fingers. Simone wasn't happy at all when Emma prolonged her exam in what was Emma's way of highlighting her unearned sense of self-importance. Emma knew I was watching. She's a smart girl.

"What the fuck?" Simone growled. "Who the hell do you think you are?"

Emma played it to the hilt. Bossy big-bosomed women don't impress me at all. In the morning, Emma would be given a visit to wardrobe and makeup as a reward for the show.

When she was done and I could almost see smoke pour from Simone's ears, Emma examined the next ass in the line. That one belonged to Chevelle, a tall North Texan who hailed from Amarillo in the panhandle. Her dark black skin set off beautiful dark eyes. Her musculature evidenced her factory-worker history. My Cop's background research showed how she progressed from shift worker to slave owner once her Domme skills became known throughout the Texas gossip line. It started with one Dallas business owner and mushroomed to include CEOs, financial advisors and as I expected, judges and politicians. It's a Texas thing.

Chevelle took no shit from anyone. But she was in dire need of more slaves to rent to her clients on days she wasn't available. Or was busy beating the crap out of a judge or a member of the legislature. Suffering through Emma's exam was a threshold she had to cross, no matter how degraded it made her feel.

"You bitch!" she barked. At least she got the gender right. "How dare you? Do you know what I can do to you with a whip?"

I'm sure Emma could guess what she could do with a whip. After all, she has tasted mine from time to time. Especially before her transformation. Gender surgery is painful and I wanted Emma to know — to feel — real pain so when her cock and balls were cut off, it wouldn't hurt quite so much.

By now, five asses passed their rectal exams. That left Danica. I had Emma do her last on purpose.

New gloves, extra lube and Emma's fingers glided into Danica. She sucked in a bit of air and stared at the blank wall inches from her blue eyes. The light caught the gold highlights in her long brown hair and she seemed to sparkle. I leaned in closer to the monitor and focused on her face.

Not one feature changed. She didn't grimace or show surprise. No, she endured the degrading exam stoically. It takes a lot to impress me and the unnecessary medical exam was designed to give me details about the Parlor guests that I couldn't get as quickly or thoroughly as the exam with Emma delivered. It's efficient. And effective.

The result was four bitchy Dommes and two who might just have earned return invitations.

When you are in Amityworld, no matter who you are or who you think you are, you obey my rules. Without protest. With gratitude.

CHAPTER 2

Domme Dressing

EMMA POINTED TO the door, sending the chagrined women to the next Intake step before they would be ushered into the Parlor building. My duo of decorators spent a personally painful day ordering and reordering chairs for the Parlor after their own asses were invaded with plugs. That's what it took for them to figure out the chair covers had to be easy to clean. Gooey residue stains would not do. They may have been surprised when I had them strip and my girl lubricated them, but there are no limits when I'm teaching a lesson. It doesn't matter who the learner is. They learn.

There was no excuse for the six Parlor guests to leave sticky dregs on the chairs, so the second Intake step was to clean them up. My girl told them to sit on the bidets in the dressing area bathroom. Bidets may sound elegant but six naked women having their asses washed together? They certainly didn't perceive sitting naked on ass washers to be a refined experience. I heard complaining from Beatrix and Chevelle, the two rural girls, but Simone and Martha dealt with the cold water through clenched teeth. At least they were quiet. Silence is one indicator of submission.

Parker, the Florida surfer, smiled and Danica wore the same patient expression she had on during her rectal exam.

They hadn't been on my property for a full hour but I already knew which two would benefit the most from the Parlor. The other four needed stricter remedial work. Given My Cop's detailed background research and the video the surveillance firm sent, I wasn't surprised with the results.

That's the thing about my Parlors. Everyone leaves knowing a lot more than when they arrived. Some lessons are more demanding than others, but they all learn. No matter how arduous the experience, every guest thanks me when they leave. Profusely.

Before sending the women to the dressing room, my girl patted their asses dry, spread their cheeks and took a long look to make sure the chairs wouldn't be soiled. Once they were dressed in their original carefully-selected Domme outfits, they would remember this grueling experience. The best way to equalize guests, from the rich or famous down to the ones on lower social or economic scales, is to have them strip. Nakedness levels them. It tells them they are all the same to me. In my world, how I regard visitors or slaves is all that matters.

I didn't bother looking at my monitors while they dressed. I could hear them clearly on the speaker. It's not easy getting Domme clothes on without chairs or benches. They struggled into their outfits and aired their grievances out loud.

"How the hell much could a couple of chairs cost?" Martha moaned. Her business is finance so her complaint didn't surprise me. If she hadn't chosen to wear 4-inch stilettos, she would have had a much easier time putting her shoes on. With her extra layers of fat and huge breasts, she grunted through lacing her bustier.

Simone was blunt. "Who does she think she is? Putting me through all of this is stupid."

Everyone knew who "she" was in Simone's rhetorical question. In her world, Simone was the boss. I guessed her employees disliked her but were too afraid to show how they really felt. She's one of those imitation Dommes who thinks that signing paychecks breeds automatic respect. By the end of the Parlor, she would realize she was wrong. Absolutely wrong. It isn't money that makes a Domme.

I listened to Chevelle's comments with interest. Her background was unique among the women in our network. She had been a factory worker, a loud and demanding one at that. She was promoted after an evening with the factory manager that included a robust spanking session, a fair amount of screaming and not just a few of his tears. I wondered if she still saw herself as a worker-bee or if she discovered the path to her authentic power.

Her remarks were short and to the point. "I did NOT enjoy this. This is NOT what I expected."

Interesting. She was all about herself and her expectations.

Chevelle didn't see herself as one of six special invitees to my Parlor. Perhaps that stemmed from her humble origins. Perhaps it was an expression of her fear that she wasn't as good as the other women whose experiences in Intake were as demeaning as hers. Either way, I kept my eye on her. I have a soft spot for women who improve their lots in life through their own hard work.

That left Parker and Danica. They were dressing quietly and never looked at the other women who were wriggling into their stockings, garter belts, stilettos and thigh-high boots while literally standing on one foot. They dressed sensibly so putting on their travel clothes in the chair-less room was a simple task. That proved a point I would emphasize in the Parlor.

Never assume. Not when you're in my world.

If a Domme learns that lesson, she can teach it to her slaves. It's a fundamental piece of building a stable. A successful, obedient stable. Keep them guessing. Lather, rinse, repeat. Pretty soon, they see the folly of trying to predict what you will do.

When they were dressed, my girl led them to the Parlor building. They walked across the grounds this time. I rode in a golf cart after they were deposited inside. Maybe next time they wouldn't wear 4- or 5-inch heels. If they were trying to impress me, that trek taught them a lesson, both physical and mental.

When I arrived, they were milling around the refreshment table, an assortment of fruit, cheese and vegetables grown in the garden by my outdoor crew. My head chef and the sous chef worked with the outdoor slaves to produce an assortment of hyper-local fruits and vegetables that complemented every meal the stable was fed. The garden provided several benefits. My feeding costs went down significantly. And the stable was never constipated.

"Welcome to the Parlor," I said casually. By ignoring what they had just been through, I told them that their strenuous introduction to my world wasn't special. Neither were they. My meaning was blunt. When you enter my world, you obey my rules. I don't care who you think you are.

That's a fundamental facet of my ownership. It doesn't matter who you are, what you own or where you come from. This is my world. I own it and everything — and everyone — in it.

If any of the women wanted to ask a question or register a

complaint, I gave them no opportunity to do so. That's another way I keep my boys and girls in line. Don't waste my time being cranky and erase any testiness from your thoughts. What you like or dislike has no place here.

"Let's get started," I said and pointed to the chairs. They finished snacking and took their seats.

The lights went down in the windowless Parlor building and the stage lights lit up the equipment on stage. Later today, they would visit my training building and the punishment out-building. The first item on my agenda was to show them how the right financial decisions help them manage their own estates successfully. Owning a stable is expensive. A few lucky Dommes' income may come from an inheritance like Parker recently acquired. Many of us rent out our slaves to supplement our income. When we buy and sell, we are always in the market for the ones with highly-rentable skills.

Then there are a few fortunate women like Danica who owned her slave's body and mind *before* he came into money. She did not choose to own him because he was wealthy, after all, that didn't happen until almost a year later. She owned him because she felt his true slave's heart.

No matter what a slave promises, a smart Domme insists upon a slave contract. I've heard too many dreadful stories of Dommes who failed to protect themselves and wound up in legal or financial trouble. Or both.

That's why I started this Parlor with a warning.

CHAPTER 3

DOMMES IN TRAINING

"EVERY SLAVE SIGNS a contract," I said. They looked at me and at each other with surprise. I'm sure they imagined I would start with a demonstration slave locked on a bench and whip his ass or another body part. They hadn't learned my rule. Yet.

Never assume when you are in my world.

"Before you take on a slave — any slave — no matter how you got him, have the slave sign your contract. Your background team should have already given you a list of the slave's financial accounts, real estate and other property. Protect yourself first."

Martha was interested. She is a financial advisor and was CFO of a fairly large company so anything related to money was in her sphere. Three of them, Simone, Beatrix and Parker, obviously had not considered the legal aspects of ownership. Poor Chevelle. There was so much to know, critical things she never learned on the factory floor. Women like her, good-hearted hard working women, don't understand the difference between money and finances.

For the first time since she had arrived, Danica looked shocked. I knew most of the details of her slave's gifts to her, most notably Destiny, including the land and all its buildings and future equipment. My Cop's task was to find out exactly who owned which parts. He said it wasn't hard to discover, no matter that it was held by a shell company or some other mysterious entity. That's another reason he's My Cop.

"Simone, tell me where your newest slave came from. How did you get him?"

She shifted her big body in the chair, buying a little time before answering. Her big breasts wobbled under her leather bustier.

"He's a rich medical type, you know, a doctor. He had a problem with his retirement accounts and was referred to me to fix it," she said.

"And he simply agreed to be your slave?" I asked.

Simone shifted again and her bosom seemed to have a mind of its own. I knew that before this Parlor was over, her breast jiggling — it had to be her tell — would show me if she understood what I taught her. Like the importance of contracts. When teaching Dommes the right way to take on a slave, I look for their tells, the little things they do that reveal their weaknesses. Simone's breasts were her giveaway.

"Well, not quite like that," she said.

Before she got the next words out, I walked to her chair, pulled her nipples out of her bustier and squeezed them with my fingers. Hard. I asked her a direct question and she did not give me a direct answer. That's not how it works in my Parlors.

I pulled her to her feet by her nipples.

"Well, like WHAT?" My tone didn't have an ounce of friendliness. My questions demand full and complete answers and the six visitors had to learn that. Now.

The other women were flummoxed. With my fingers gripping Simone's nipples and her grunting in pain, they dared not interrupt out of fear my next lesson would be theirs.

Simone stammered as much from shock as from pain. Finally, she found her words.

"He … he said he should be spanked for investing poorly. I said he was correct. Right then, I had him drop his pants — he wasn't wearing any underwear — and put him across my knees."

Even though that was a more complete reply, a single spanking does not create a slave. But Simone had one advantage. She knew his complete financial picture. I didn't have to ask whether she had him sign over any of it to her. I was sure it never occurred to her.

"How much of his wealth is yours now?"

I stepped back, still crushing her nipples. When she stepped toward me, I walked toward the stage, dragging her on those stupid stilettos.

"None," she confessed.

That was the right answer. She had a play toy, not a slave. A doctor who liked getting his ass spanked would use her to fulfill his fantasy when he felt like it. All she had to show for her work with him was her hourly consulting fee. That doesn't pay for a slave's upkeep. Or her own.

I let go of her nipples and pointed to her chair. The big arrogant woman plopped into it, her face red and her bosom sore. My stare made her drop her hands to her sides. There is no nipple rubbing in my Parlor.

I turned my attention to Beatrix, a Domme whose income came primarily from paid dominatrix work. Her blonde hair and green eyes certainly didn't hurt her from getting paying clients. But paying clients take care of today. What about tomorrow?

"Stand up," I said.

Simone was still moaning, so Beatrix weighed her options and stood up. Quickly.

"How do your clients reserve your time?" I asked. It was an easy question. I already knew the answer.

"An online calendar," she said. "They get a link. They make an appointment."

Inexperienced Dommes permit clients to make appointments. Skilled ones allow clients to *request* time. Beatrix had to learn who worked for whom. My Cop had already seen her calendar system and raised his concerns.

"Using tools that any idiot can get online, I know your full name, address, phone and have seen your tax records. Did you not think to add a password to the site, at the least? Or do you allow just anyone to book your time?"

"Oh god," she mumbled. It was fine for her to be upset but it was not fine that she didn't answer my question. She had set herself up for disaster and needed to take immediate steps to correct it. That required a serious lesson.

I don't enjoy humiliating Dommes. If that's the only way they learn, so be it. In a case like this, the end does justify my means.

"Simone's nipples are sore. Get on your knees and suck them."

Four bemused women stared at the floor. Simone's eyes turned to Beatrix and Beatrix's were focused on me. Her face was red. I could sense her insides were roiling with indecision. Yet her entire future from the upcoming auction to being accepted into our network was at stake. Beatrix soon realized her only option was in my hands.

She knelt in front of Simone, pulled one nipple between her lips and sucked. Some lessons are difficult to learn. Others are onerous.

While Beatrix sucked, I turned my attention to Martha. I didn't need time to figure out what her weakness was. It was obvious. Her black eyes tried not to meet mine so I put my finger under her chin and tilted her face up. She was shaking and I hadn't asked her a question. Yet.

"What does it cost you to keep one in-house slave?"

That should have been easy for her to answer. Martha knows money and has to know the cost of everything in her household. Every Domme has to be intimately familiar with her expenses and make sure her income at least covers her costs. Keeping a stable is expensive.

Although Simone's breasts were fairly large, they dwarfed in comparison to Martha's. But unlike Simone, the short woman's bosom wasn't her weakness. I saw her tell when she stripped in Intake. Short, heavy women share the same quirk.

Beatrix answered confidently. "I have a small building that houses both of my slaves. With heat and lights, that's $350/month per slave. A third one will reduce that cost per slave."

She tried to smile, trusting she had answered my question. It was time to dispel her of that mistake.

"So you starve them?" I asked.

"Oh no! I feed them."

She still had not given me a complete answer. In addition to food, they have occasional medical expenses, tools they use for the work she assigns them and the insurance she buys for the property. My Cop provided complete records because I never ask questions if I don't know the answers. I learned that from my lawyers and My Cop learned it from me. And his lifetime in law enforcement.

"How much in *total*?" I demanded.

Beatrix's eyes were wet. She was almost panicking, trying to add and subtract in her head. Numbers, something she prides herself on, failed her. I was done waiting for her to give me the single number I asked for.

"Take off your skirt," I said evenly. I watched her dress earlier. She wasn't wearing panties, just a garter belt and black hose.

Martha's eyes were begging me not to debase her in front of the other women but if a Domme can't answer a simple question that every slave owner should have at the tip of her fingers, then she needs to be taught. Intimately. I tapped my foot.

Martha unzipped her custom-made black leather skirt and stepped out of it. I tossed it aside.

"Sit and spread your knees," I said. To her credit, she obeyed. A jolt from my small prod deep inside her big thighs was greeted by loud screeches. Then I did it again. Like I said, some lessons are painful. Pain with a purpose fosters faster learning.

That brought me to Chevelle, the woman I was most concerned about, save for Danica who was another story. I wanted Chevelle to succeed, especially because she started out with nothing and I wanted her to have not just something, but more than that. She deserved a comfortable lifestyle but had to earn it first. That meant long-term schooling on the difference between money and finances. At 5'11" and strong as an ox, Chevelle's earning potential from paying clients was enormous. She needed three things before that could happen: more paying clients, a place to use them and profit from her work.

Her dark eyes were filled with fear and followed me when I stood in front her chair. I bet she hadn't felt dread like this in a long time. She pulled herself out of poverty and loved the taste of success. Even minor success like the life she had now.

Before I asked her a question, I tapped Martha's pussy again. Twice. Her screams encouraged Chevelle to reply quickly. It didn't matter what the question was. She knew she had to answer.

"How many whips do you own and how much do they cost?" I asked. Then I added, "Plus the cost of sterilizing tools."

She didn't expect a question that specific. It took her breath away. This tall, strong woman was reduced to a shuddering mass of flesh from a simple question. Women like her are used to controlling situations through physical intimidation. That doesn't work with me.

After all, I have My Cop. And when he's working remotely, I keep my protection dog, Aussie, close at hand. Rather, close to my feet. Aussie was a gift from Maeve and Annalise, the owners of the <u>Femdom Pet Shoppe</u>. Aussie is exceptionally well trained. My Cop trains him. And I train My Cop.

Chevelle was literally shaking in her thigh-high boots. Either she had no idea what her whips cost, or worse, she wasn't sterilizing them.

Either result was unacceptable. I wanted more for her and whatever it took to teach her how to get it, well, that's how she was going to learn.

I tapped my foot. Chevelle's eyes filled with tears. No, not in my Parlor. There are no weeping Dommes allowed. I could tell she was desperate to answer but had no words. No matter, I had the solution for the ones who cry.

"If you want to cry, I'll give you something to cry about. Turn around and bend over."

Chevelle turned, bent over the chair and held onto the back. I held my left hand out and my girl put a rattan cane in it. I pointed and she lifted Chevelle's skirt up to her waist. A solid dark-skinned set of asscheeks greeted me. When training slaves or Dommes, there's no time like the present. Four swings later, Chevelle had something real to cry about. Before leaving her bent over and her legs spread, I tapped Martha again as a reminder, then landed two crisscross strokes on Chevelle's backside and walked to where Parker and Danica were sitting.

To their credit, they both looked directly at me. They didn't turn their heads like scared chickens. I put Parker on the spot first.

When Emma examined her rectum, I saw Parker smile. It was a small smile, but she was the only Domme whose lips turned upward. If a rectal exam made her smile, she deserved a rectal question.

"I know you don't want slaves with damaged rectums. They're useless. Tell me how you check for unspoiled asses."

It was a good bet that Parker did not have the equipment to do an internal check. Cameras on flexible arms are expensive and I didn't see that kind of cash in her financials. In fact, I was certain she failed to check any of her stock for anal tears or rectal scarring. When I consider buying a slave, his ass is as important as the length of his cock. I'll purchase one with a short cock if he has skills I need and rentable talents. But never an injured ass. They aren't useful at all.

Parker had no answer. She had never been told to examine anuses so she had no idea she should even look at them. I appreciated that she didn't lie to me. Had she lied, she'd find herself deposited at the airport for the trip home. She looked at me, actually past me, searching for something to say. There was only one reply she could give and earn any respect from me.

"I didn't know," she said. "There's a lot I don't know."

That was perfect. And it was exactly what I'd show her when she returned for a follow-up Parlor. I handed her my rattan cane and told her to whack Chevelle's asscheeks while I moved to the last Domme in the audience.

Chevelle shrieked after each stroke. It was music to my ears.

CHAPTER 4

Danica's Question

DANICA LOOKED NERVOUS when I approached her and for good reason. Four of the five previous women failed to meet what I consider a fundamental level of competence in bringing new slaves into their households. They were destined to become those appalling stories we have all heard about failed Dommes. We had a name for them. They were the "poor girls" on my network's video calls. They didn't even merit being called "Dommes."

When I read through the applications for this Parlor, I could foresee disasters in several of their futures. That could be avoided if they were willing to learn the hard facts about owning slaves and running a household. I was willing to teach them the ins, outs and secrets but only if they were willing to do the work.

Danica was one of the rare ones who had a devoted slave with the wealth and commitment to gift her the land, buildings and tools of her dreams. Those are physical things, important things, but things nonetheless. Unless she knew how to manage all of it and at the same time make sure she had solid recurring revenue, all those things made no difference. She called it "Destiny" and I wanted it to be hers for a long time.

The slave she brought was in Intake being examined by Emma and attended to by the estheticians. I agreed to let him keep his head hair at Danica's request, even though there wasn't a lot there. But not the rest. That had to go. He was given a temporary cot in a small room off the Intake building because Jack didn't need a hairy slave to deal with. The boy had no experience being just one of many owned boys and I would not tolerate any disruption. Nova, my personal female, was instructed to alert me if he caused any trouble.

I had plans for Danica's slave to be used as a demo later in this Parlor. Danica planned to buy more so it was important for her to see how her boy reacted to being exhibited and used.

All the women attending this Parlor wanted bigger stables, more slaves, more tools, more prestige in our small but exclusive community. That's why I agreed to teach them that having more of those things did not automatically grant them our respect. They were finding out that to understand what respect is, they had to suffer through their own degradation. With pinched nipples being sucked, a vagina receiving electric jolts and an ass being whipped with a rattan cane, they learned what being disrespected feels like. Personally. This all-day Parlor would show them that respect from me, and through my recommendations, our network's respect, is not given freely. They had to pay the price. They were paying it right now. In spades.

It is a high price to pay. But what they get in return is a lifelong education.

Danica kept eye contact with me even though she was nervous about my question and possibly suffering punishment if she failed to answer correctly. Uneasiness flowed behind her stoic face. I chose my question specifically for her.

"When you buy another slave, how will you train the one you have to be your second? What will you do to show him he is no longer that important to you?"

Apparently from her quick inhale, Danica didn't anticipate my question would be that personal. Owners have to be careful when they grow their property. You may not realize you are favoring one over another and even though it's your right, a neglected slave can become disruptive. This slave bought Destiny for Danica and she had to make sure it was all in her name. You never know what lawyers can write into contracts until a better lawyer reviews it.

If her boy felt abandoned, would she lose her Destiny?

Her answer would tell me what she knew for certain about her ownership of the land and the boy. It goes without saying that I knew who owned the land and the buildings on it. Her future depended on how she would train her slave to accept his new, lower status.

In my world, My Cop and Zayn are my exclusives. They live in cells in the attic of the main house, not in the dorm with the stable. The two of them are the only slaves allowed in my rooms and I use them for my sensual satisfaction. In fact, My Cop is the only slave allowed to keep his head hair. Because I like it that way.

If my stable has a problem with how I treat my exclusives, they learn at the tip of my single-tail it is not their concern. My slaves are kept hairless and naked in cock cages and are milked three times each week to keep them in check. They complete daily physical fitness routines, perform work on the grounds and in my businesses and are rented to my elite clients to satisfy the clients' kinks and fetishes. In return, my slaves are grateful to be allowed to live in Amityworld. They know it is a privilege to be owned by me and if they fail to perform or please me, they will be expelled.

It's rare that I expel a slave, but when I do, he leaves with what he brought with him. A thin gray jumpsuit, a bus ticket, his IDs and nothing else. My boys have witnessed an expulsion and they vowed it would never happen to them. In fact, when they age and are no longer of use, I send them to a remote facility where they are cared for and occasionally whipped to remind them of the good life they once enjoyed.

Did Danica's slave comprehend that he was to become merely one of her slaves? That her holdings would grow and his place was wherever she put him?

Danica stood up and faced me.

"My slave is devoted to me, body and mind. But you're right, he has no competition. Can you show me how to teach him that even though he has been generous, it does not make him special?"

She couldn't have said anything better than that. I was teaching Dommes in this Parlor something she already knew. Those women just learned that if you don't know the answer, ask the right person the right question and learn.

I looked at Beatrix on her knees sucking Simone's nipples, Martha moaning from repeated pussy jolts and Parker striping Chevelle's asscheeks. They would keep at it until I told them to stop. They were learning obedience and could now teach it to their slaves. The best lessons are taught hands-on.

"Get dressed, we have slave contracts to discuss."

I sent a girl to fetch my dog, Aussie. With My Cop working remotely for several weeks, I keep my dog at my feet for protection.

Protection was a good idea because the next agenda item for the Parlor would test these women beyond anything they had been put through before.

Slave Contracts

CHAPTER 5

CREATING CONTRACTS

LAWYERS ARE A DREADFUL lot. Until you need one. I engaged two law firms years ago to protect me and my property, including my stable. It was surprisingly easy to find a full-service law firm and a solo practitioner who were open to my lifestyle and specific needs. One of them is led by a woman who could easily be a Domme and I was careful not to push her beyond her limits. At first.

That changed the day I bought the bastard in Sweden, the one who outed my friend and caused her years of legal trouble and emotional agony. I am still convinced his maliciousness led to her untimely death. I pledged to punish him if I ever got my hands on him. When he was put up for sale in Sweden, I bought him in pre=sales without haggling over the price. After he was delivered, I had him locked in a tiny cage where he lived alone and was forced to listen to the testimony against him on an audio loop. That lawyer asked to see the conditions I kept him in. I'm sure she wanted to make sure I didn't intend to kill him. Heck, I didn't want him dead. I wanted him to suffer. No one ever stared at a monitor as intensely as she did.

After two years of daily whippings, cleaning toilets and muck from sunup to dark, I had him castrated and sold him to an Asian master with an unusual kink. The only condition on the sale was that I would never hear from or about him again.

The lesson he learned was clear-cut. Never fuck with my friends. I keep his balls in a jar.

Bringing new slaves into your stable is a process. In my world, my background research firm provides video and audio recordings of them at work, at home and at play. I review what My Cop discovers and listen to his take on whether or not the candidate is the type I want. More recently, Zayn's input has been valuable. He is my second exclusive and my Tantric guide. Zayn has the rare ability to sense another person's spirit. A simple nod or headshake is all I need from him to know what he detects. Zayn's only longing is to be near me, to feel his own essence that the old Asian Master taught him to cede to me to hold. Zayn's primary job is to satisfy my overpowering needs and he does that whenever I summon him. Many of those nights don't end until the sun rises. My nights — and days —are amazing. My needs don't follow a clock.

Zayn and My Cop blend together well. Once the tip of my single-tail kisses his ass, My Cop morphs into a driving force whose only purpose is to stoke and feed my hunger. Zayn ignites my fire and makes it burn. My Cop sets it ablaze.

As for the rest of the herd, they are happy to be owned. Their lives are simple and their time is accounted for, down to the minute. The schedule gives them three times every day to piss-and-shit, they eat healthy meals and are seen weekly by my doctor. When I rent them to clients, they understand they are serving me. They work hard so they are requested frequently by number. Slaves are grateful for the few minutes their cock cages are unlocked three times a week when they are machine milked.

No slave ejaculates unless I have a specific purpose for it. The boys I keep have microchips implanted in their perineums that I can engage from anywhere. You can tell when I press their button. Look for the male on the ground, shrieking in pain. I never have to explain what a boy did wrong. He knows. He learns to treat chip pain as a correction and never breaks that rule again out of the fear I will expel him. Likewise for the rest of the boys after they see one writhing in agony on the floor.

Before I take in a slave, whether I buy him or he applies, he signs a contract. My slave contracts are as simple as they are complicated. That's what lawyers are for.

Simply put, everything a slave owns, from furniture to clothing, is donated to a charity. His financial accounts and real estate holdings are signed over to my company. A slave arrives naked wearing only a thin gray jumpsuit and his identification is locked in a vault. When a slave leaves, he takes what he brought. Almost nothing.

There are three ways a slave can leave. I can sell him outright or trade him for another one. Old ones are retired to a remote holding facility. The third option is expulsion. Slavery is forever and a good slave contract makes that clear. Perfectly clear.

The six Dommes in the Parlor building were about to see the dangers of contract-less slaves. The women were mostly recovered from learning what total degradation feels like. Their next challenge would cover the steps in drawing up unbreakable slave contracts. That step is the first rung on the ladder to being accepted into our network. Dommes' chattel has to be bound to them, legally and by the slave's choice. There is nothing that makes a Domme slip down that ladder faster than by having belligerent or confrontational property. A Domme's reputation is built in large part by the quality of her stock. Solid contracts are the underpinnings of well-trained slaves. The way slaves look and act are reflections of your ownership.

I had the women sit around a table with blank paper and pens. We do not write contracts in pencil.

"None of you currently has slave contracts on file with your attorneys," I said. That piece of information was almost too easy for me to uncover. "That changes today." I didn't tell them it was My Cop who exposed their failure.

If the six women were surprised, they didn't show it. In fact, they looked like sponges, eager to absorb effective ways to guard their property, both the land and the creatures who inhabit it.

"Write down the three most important items you think are necessary for a slave contract. Think about the time *before* they arrive. That's what the contract has to include. Once they are in your stable, it's too late to have them sign a contract."

They picked up the pens but no one wrote a word. They were thinking. Hard. Running scenarios through their heads. Remembering how they bought their newest slave. Imagining where they would find new ones. I let them stew for several minutes before they finally came up with lists on the notepaper. I had a feeling their lists would be woefully inadequate.

I'm usually right about situations like this. I was this time, too.

"Parker, read me your list," I said. I chose her to go first because she seemed to have a level head and a lovely piece of property she planned to use for rentals.

"My first is to make sure boys I buy say they are entering slavery willingly. That they want to be owned. By me."

My opinion of Parker rose a notch. Her first list item is the most basic one to ownership. A boy has to give himself voluntarily to *you*. If he is coerced, then nothing else in your contract holds water.

"That's critical," I said. "You nailed that one."

The other women at the table scribbled furiously on their paper. At least four of them omitted that vital step. I moved down the line.

Beatrix's knees were probably still sore from kneeling and sucking Simone's nipples. I hoped that didn't distract her from coming up with useful rules for her contract.

"Beatrix, you are working as a Domme for hire. That's where most of your income comes from. You have specific needs in a contract. Read your first one to me now."

"It's about money, Beatrix said. "How much I charge for a session has to be in the contract."

She actually smirked after reading that ridiculous clause aloud.

"Congratulations! That's the fastest way to be sent to jail. In some states, that's a prostitution clause. Rethink that before I put you on your knees again, lapping whatever I tell you to suck."

"Well?" I asked.

Beatrix was mouthing words, trying to put a sentence together. Finally, she came up with a reply.

"Um, I think something about getting hurt?"

"You think? You THINK? You have to *know*."

'Yes, a medical clause has to be in the contract." At least she got that right. A good lawyer can handle the exact wording.

The other women hurriedly added that one to their lists. It was stunning they didn't include possible injury in the first place. The next Domme I put on the spot was Martha. When I called on her, she moved her arm from between her thighs where she was probably rubbing her sore pussy and put her hand on the table. I made a mental note to have my girls sanitize everything in the Parlor building. Twice.

"Martha, is there an item on your list that you can connect to having your pussy kissed by my prod? Surely, that episode is still fresh in your mind. And elsewhere."

I didn't have to smile. The women at the table did it for me. Martha was the only one whose lips turned down. She took a deep breath and said, "A slave has to know I will punish him. He must accept that as a condition."

Well, well. You *can* teach a Domme new tricks. Of course a slave has to accept punishment but more than that, he has to *want* it. In fact, the ones who crave it are the some of the best ones to buy. You can find lots of boys like that for sale at our auctions and even more in online inventories.

"Your premise is right, that a slave has to know he will be beaten, whipped and degraded. It's not a condition, though. It's the way of life for every boy you own."

I saw the women write that stipulation on their paper. That left Chevelle and Danica. Chevelle was shifting on the hard chair. Her ass still stung from the rattan cane Parker wielded on her cheeks. There was something about Chevelle that made me want to see her grow. I am partial to hard luck stories and I like happy endings.

"Chevelle, you are currently using boys who contact you to schedule time. I'm sure you know there are dozens, if not hundreds of men who will pay handsomely for that service. Given that you don't have your own facility yet, what's on your list?"

Chevelle budged in the chair and said, "They have to keep my secrets."

There was hope for Chevelle, too. Although she didn't say it elegantly, her point was valid.

"Absolutely!" I said. Chevelle's full lips broke into a smile. If she could not get respect from her factory work, then she could get it from her power over men higher up the food chain. "Absolute discretion. A binding NDA. Forever. That has to be in every slave contract or the results can be disastrous. For you. It's never the men who get pilloried in the newspaper or online. It will be you."

Their pens were on fire, adding more rules to their contracts.

"Danica, your situation is different. Tell me what is on your list, especially related to your new property."

Danica stood up, held her paper with both hands and faced me.

"Ms. Amity, what I take from a slave becomes mine. Forever. Even if I throw him out."

Game. Set. Match.

When Danica stood up, I knew what she was saying without words. Using my name properly was a bonus. Danica showed respect and that is the next rung on the ladder to being accepted by my circle of friends. Her rule about owning a slave's possessions was inspired.

"If that's not on your list, put it there right now." Five pens were working overtime.

-=o=-

Now that they had the basics of a slave contract, it was time to show the women how a contract works with actual slaves. I jolted Jack's chip and she scurried in with six boys jogging behind her. When I summon slaves, they don't walk. They run.

Jack led the boys to the stage, locked their wrists to the overhead bar and strapped a spreader between their ankles. The boys I chose for this demonstration ran the gamut from almost new to ones with their numbers tattooed on their asses, a sign that I intend to keep them. At least for a while. Slaves don't need names. I have numbers tattooed on their right asscheek. They are much easier for me to see there.

"Now that you have a better idea of what has to be included in a slave contract, I want you to see examples of what that agreement means. Go up on the stage and stand in front of a boy. One Domme per slave."

Martha, Beatrix and Chevelle walked up the steps to the stage and eyed each boy. They didn't own stables yet; they used boys one at a time as needed. I am not sure the three of them had seen a female slave before, especially one like Jack who was dressed in her display leathers, the outfit my girls wear when I have company. Crotchless leather shorts, a bustier that ends just under their breasts and thigh-high boots are what I call their dress clothes.

Parker and Simone figured out that tattooed boys must be special in some way so they each chose to stand in front of one of them. That left Danica to select her slave. She wound up in front of the newest boy in the stable, a 6'2" muscular specimen with several rentable skills and a particularly long cock.

The women gaped at their crotches. My boys stared at me.

"These are your instructions. No boy will speak unless you ask him a question. His answer will be short and to the point. Slaves are not allowed to engage in casual conversation. Make your questions clear and easy to answer to get the information you want."

I looked down the line of boys and the backs of the women facing them. My boys didn't see those women. They looked past them at me. For the boys, the only thing an unfamiliar face means is that they may be handed off to them, temporarily or worse, permanently. None of these demos wanted to be sold and all of them would work their asses off if I handed them off and told them to satisfy these women right now. My boys do not perform merely adequately for the women or men I rent or give them to. They perform exceptionally. It's one of the clauses in their contracts. They know the consequences.

First, my whip. Last, a thin gray jumpsuit and a bus ticket.

"You may ask the boy three questions to find out how — and in what ways — the contracts they signed affect them every day."

If they thought getting answers would be easy, they were about to learn a lot about what rules are in my contracts. I hoped the women were smart enough to learn some of those conditions with intelligent questions.

Jack did a sound check in her earbuds to make sure the questions and answers were recorded. In fact, that is also a stipulation in my contracts. Slaves are monitored by microphones and video cameras at all times. A few of them who already signed over their extensive holdings to my companies bristled at being recorded. Once my attorney informed them that recordings were required and if they refused to sign, they had already ceded their possessions to me. They signed the contracts and submitted to 24/7 monitoring. They didn't have to like it. What they like is unimportant. That's what their signatures validated. That's what their slavery continues to mean.

I only accept slaves who understand what my power over them entails. From the most basic bodily functions to every minute of their days, I own them. That's what I wanted the women interrogating my demo slaves to find out. Hopefully, one or two of them were astute enough to dig it out of them.

Simone asked #57, a 5'10" tattooed piece of my landscape crew, what he gave up to live as a slave. I noticed she did not ask what he gave up to live as a slave in *my* stable. That was her mistake. #57 was a boy I bought from Nashville Ned, a seller who reminds us constantly that he buys and sells only first-quality merchandise. Aside from his daily work on the grounds, they boy is a frequent rental, especially to groups where his expertly-trained mouth satisfies their fantasies one after another.

He looked for my nod, permission to speak, before he dared reply. "Everything," he said.

Simone needed to ask better questions. She followed up with, "What is the best part of being a slave?"

He looked for another nod before answering. "Everything."

Again, she left out a crucial piece of the question. She should have asked, "What is the best part of being *Ms. Amity's* slave?" That would have told her much more about what I told her to find out. Given Simone's arrogant attitude toward her slaves and to most people in general, she lacked the insight to know a slave's heart. My slave's heart. Simone's grilling went nowhere.

Beatrix, the athletic Colorado Domme, interviewed #89, a small boy whose skills were in technology. I bought him in Memphis to produce videos for the marketing girls. My clients choose what they want to rent after seeing them in action. Short videos on my private site generate repeated rental requests. But #89 was fairly new to my stable and her green eyes peered through his, all the way into his gut. I hoped she asked better questions than Simone. Heck, almost any questions would be better than hers.

#89 wasn't simply naked. I hadn't chipped him yet, so he wore an anal plug he knew could torture him for misbehavior. One drop of gel from the plug would send him into agony. The new plugs that drip into a boy's ass have become a quick way to show a slave why total obedience is better than, well, anything less.

"How does having your owner control everything you do every day, down to the last detail like when you can pee, make you feel?"

I almost laughed. This little IT worker grew up with an old-school German nanny regulating his life, including checking the toilet after he used it. Being owned was the only life he knew. He couldn't survive without it.

When I nodded, he answered. "Comforting."

Of course he was comfortable here! He had the tech tools he longed for and his ass was busy at least three nights each week. His nanny owned it for years. Now I do.

The Dommes' interviews went on like that. They received almost none of the useful information I told them to get. Certainly nothing they could add to their slave contracts, the actual purpose of the exercise.

Martha asked what the boy would tell his owner if she allowed him to speak freely. #40 was one of two space planners I picked up in Houston that I used when I redesigned the out-buildings into cabins for long-term rentals. When I told him to sketch a perfect punishment building, he couldn't have been happier. The results reflect his talent. Even better, #40 is one of my top screamers. That skill meshes nicely with his fetish to be at the business end of my whip. Screamers are many of my most repeated requests. That's one reason I had some out-buildings remodeled. No one hears them through the soundproofing. Besides, they were built way across the fields.

He looked for my nod and then said, "I am not free. I do not speak freely."

So much for Martha's big bosom and jiggling fat.

The boy Chevelle chose was one of my big ones. At 6'6" with an 8.25" cock when it's soft, I use him as the stable's trainer. After selling my bull, the slave who did not win the bullfight in Memphis, I bought #51 from the Spanish Dommes I met at the Swedish Auction. They bought him as an investment, bulked him up and put him on sale. My Cop's research revealed he was former military, always a plus on my rating scale. He was a Marine, through and through. Zayn sensed his obedience when he helped drain his combativeness. Just a little. I had plans to have him trained and offer him to the Femdom Pet Shoppe owners. He was born to be a pit bull.

I was sure Chevelle chose him because of his size. She was about to learn that good things do not have to come in big packages.

"What are your most important two duties as a slave?" she asked.

I nodded. I was interested in what he had to say.

"Obedience," he said without a second's hesitation. Then he added, "Fidelity."

Spoken like a true marine. Kept naked, cock-caged and chipped didn't diminish his commitment to me one bit. It enhanced it.

Chevelle looked at him quizzically but his eyes were focused on me. When I nodded, he closed his eyes and dropped his chin to his chest. An experienced Domme would have recognized that immediately as an act of submission to his owner.

Even if Chevelle didn't understand the depth of his answer, I did. My simple nod launched ripples across his massive muscles. I sent a few seconds of the pleasure program to his chip and he took a little trip for those seconds. Maybe I would keep him, at least for a while.

If any of the women were going to ask useful questions, it was up to Parker and Danica. Parker had one of my long-term slaves but Danica's was new. I chose #34 as a demo because I'd had him for three years, almost a lifetime in ownership years. I keep him because he is my most regular rental. The fees I charge pay for his own upkeep, of course, and also cover three more slaves. Some weeks, the revenue he brings in is higher than that.

I had his ass was tattooed two years ago. I had his cock done recently. Numbers help me remember what to call the boys. With the big #34 on his shaft and right asscheek, I can find his number no matter which way he is kneeling.

#34 has an unusual skill. A former actor, he is a believable role-player. My clients are the elite class in business, politics, diplomacy, and medicine. They are desperate to give up the control they have to wield every day and #34 is the perfect solution. Whether they want a school teacher, police officer, nurse or any other authority figure, #34 becomes it. He's trained to use small whips and other tools that make it easy to lay a governor or CEO across his knees. His fitness routine developed his arms so his open-hand spanking makes the most prosperous men cry. They bawl. They beg to come back for more.

Parker asked, "I know your owner gives you food and shelter. Aside from that, what is the most important thing your owner gives you?"

If I were keeping score, Parker just got a +1.

I nodded. He said, "Ms. Amity owns me, body and mind. It's the greatest gift."

Even though #34 can assume any personality my clients want, I knew what he said was genuine. I bought him from Red Rick three years ago. It's a shame that #34 will never be allowed to serve my personal needs, but I'm sure he will do that for someone. Someone else. Whenever I sell him.

Parker had the answer she needed for her slave contract. I planned to have her tell me how she would incorporate his reply into it. If she could, she would recoup at least the cost of keeping her slaves.

Danica was next. As much as I wanted to hear her questions, I wanted to know why she chose that boy.

#99 was newly depilated, newly plugged and newly mine. I took him for an important reason, one I wasn't sure she was savvy enough to drag out of him.

CHAPTER 6

DANICA'S QUESTIONS

I DON'T BUY SEXLESS slaves. For a boy to be interesting, my first test is to see if he wags his tail when I approach. If it stands up, I'll take a closer look. Sexual boys are easier to train. Once they are locked in cock cages, they submit almost immediately. If they assume I will unlock them at some point for their own enjoyment, they are wrong. Male slaves are usually wrong when they think they can predict what I will do.

#99 was a different story. During the pandemic, I took in only a few boys, mostly other Dommes' property, to repair or rehabilitate and ship them back to their owners. All on a commission basis. I like getting paid to do what I already enjoy doing. This boy was one I worked with during that time.

He did not arrive through the typical route. My Cop sent him.

Due to his position, My Cop was vaccinated in the first group. He begged for an hour of my time and flew in when I agreed to his unusual request. Right then, I knew whoever or whatever the boy was, he was special. My Cop has never asked for anything except my ownership, so I was more than a little intrigued. Once I met the boy on a video call where I could see him but all he could see on his monitor was my big *A* icon, I knew he would be mine. Eventually. After he retired from the military. He could serve as a worthwhile remote until he put in his papers. Then I would own him. All of him.

I am partial to military types. They are absolutely obedient on their first day here so when I start their training, they are at least a week or more ahead of typical ones. I rarely have to send ex-military slaves to the punishment building for correction like I do the regular ones.

Those boys have to learn my rules. This boy submitted to me instantly.

He didn't need to be corrected or punished. What he needed was the intimacy of my ownership and the kiss of my single-tail on his ass.

Pain with a purpose works wonders.

He had been a prisoner of war, officially a POW, and fought like hell to keep his sanity until he was rescued. That was how he met My Cop, the operative who led the covert team that brought him home. Once he was stateside, he looked and acted like a regular officer and even the shrinks he had to meet with were taken in by his bravado. Medals were awarded, promotions bestowed. Yet he held a heartbreaking secret from all of them, including himself.

Until My Cop sent him to me.

Unwrapping his secret was painful. He was miles past mortified when I forced him to confess what he was hiding. He was doubly humiliated that I already knew his secret, that I figured out his ultimate shame so easily.

The horror left him impotent.

Prison was hell and to survive, he created a world inside his head, a safe place where he could escape the reality of the small bamboo cage that wasn't tall enough for him to stand. The beatings. The starvation. He never spoke to his captors, save for his name, rank and serial number. He never revealed the information they tortured him to divulge. He was grateful to be alive even if it meant keeping his impotence secret from everyone. He lived alone. Both physically and mentally.

He arrived one night in the transport garage, naked but proud. His useless cock didn't wag when I stood next to him. My Cop pleaded with me to spend one hour with him, the only thing he has ever asked me to do for him. I spent two days with the boy and when I was done, the soldier sobbed at my feet with gratitude.

My Cop was grateful even though he didn't know — will *never* know — the details. So grateful that, for the first time since he gave himself to me and I took him, he wept.

Breaking boys is easy most of the time. Not this boy, not this time. I didn't demand he submit to me by leaps and bounds, no, he was inch by inch. When I was done with him, he didn't want to leave. I told him he could return but only when he was ready.

I had My Cop take him back to his outside world until he was prepared to pledge his life to me. A few weeks ago, the boy asked to speak to me and My Cop used the number I set up for him to contact Nova, my new personal female. She crawled into my office and delivered his request.

An hour later, the boy's body filled my monitors. All of them. 360-degree floor-to-ceiling visuals of him, naked from head to toe. When I said, "Speak," his cock shot up.

That's what pain with a purpose can do.

Now he was #99, standing on stage and enduring his first time being used as one of my demos. It's one thing to be a decorated military officer. It is quite another to be one of six naked males, facing a woman who wasn't me.

Danica was ready with her questions. I was iffy about what he might say. Would he rise to her interrogation? Or would the awful memories return?

"Why did you sign Ms. Amity's contract?" she asked.

I held my breath. Then I saw his eyes and I wasn't concerned. Not one bit. #99's eyes lit up when I nodded.

He said, "Because this is where I am supposed to be. Where I WANT to be!"

His cock jiggled up and down, like a bouncing exclamation point.

Danica's next question was as well thought-out as mine would have been had I been in her position. "Can Ms. Amity trust you?"

He saw me nod and said, "I would die before I would ever violate Ms. Amity's trust."

I knew that was true. He proved his faithfulness when he was in that damned prisoner camp. My Cop told me the whole ugly story.

Danica had one question left and I was curious what she would ask. "Who are you?"

I was gripping my whip handle so hard, my nails were leaving marks on my palm but I managed to nod one more time.

"MS. AMITY OWNS ME!" he shouted.

His cock jumped up. Full staff. Danica nodded at him but #99 was staring at me.

"Yes, I do," I said. "For as long as I want you."

Tears ran down his face and damn, I needed a tissue. I love it when a plan comes together.

Remotes and Applicants

CHAPTER 7

APPLICANTS

I BUY SLAVES. Sometimes I trade for them. It's a rare occasion that I take one that applies. I have methods to evaluate for-sale boys when it's a one-to-one video call with a seller. Auctions require a different approach that I put to use in <u>Sweden</u> and <u>Memphis</u>. Trading with reputable Dommes and Old Leather Masters like Big Mike or sellers like Nashville Ned means I rely on trust and the seller's reputation. I let them know what I'm looking for and what I have available to barter. If they have a match, the transaction takes place and Red Rick takes care of the shipping.

Once in a while when I'm bored with my stable, I make an application available for boys to submit their complete histories, photos and a video statement, for my consideration. The video is the boy's confession of his lifelong quest for ownership. A boy gets two-minutes to make me interested in him. He tells me why I want him and explains in detail what he can do for me.

They know what I will give them. The privilege of living in Amityworld for as long as I care to keep them.

Most applications are rejected before I listen to the end. They're wannabees. Overly effusive. Dishonest. Too old, too young. I am very selective. Brielle, the Mistress of the Atlanta-area Maison, says I am picky. She's right.

When I see an interesting applicant, my first order of business is a background check that My Cop handles. He has ways of finding things that regular people are not privy to. Like criminal records, even if they're hidden or expunged. Military service and what kind of discharge the boy was awarded. Medical information that might disqualify a boy from the hard work my slaves do.

Once I delete the unacceptable ones, I look at the remaining few in more detail. Do they have the skills I need and want? I never take a boy with only one talent. If I have use for, say, an accountant, he has to be rentable often enough that he covers my costs to keep him. Uncovering a boy's second skill often shows up in a video interview.

Like I said, taking applicants into my stable is a long, thorough and demanding process. I have a plethora of demands.

There is a lot I can tell from applications and videos. But when I have the boy live on camera, his *self* is available to me. While he sees the big *A* icon on his screen, I have a 360-degree view of him in every room of his home or apartment. My surveillance team does quality work.

What do I look for in an applicant on camera? First, of course, is his body. Is he fit or fat? Strong or a weakling who needs to spend time building up his muscles? Stiff or can he bend over and spread his cheeks for the camera? Then there is the cock. I want to see if it stiffens or lays there like a mushroom. Sexual boys are easier to train.

After I run him through obedience tests and listen to the quality and volume of his grunts and groans, I know if he's a screamer. There are only so many of those I want in the stable. They can be noisy.

If the applicant passes my visual inspection, I put him on his knees and ask challenging questions. Very personal ones. I can sense if a boy is being truthful and if he's not, one click ends the call. I do not explain. It's a simple rule. Never lie to me. You will not like what happens to the ones that do.

A random applicant rarely gets all the way through my tests, but if one does, Nova arranges for him to be delivered to my transport garage in one of Red Rick's windowless trucks. That boy is not sent through regular Intake but Emma examines him, top to bottom, inside and out. I usually watch the exam and at the first sign of noncompliance, he is sent back to transport for a trip to a bus station an hour-and-a-half away with a one-way ticket. Rejects are clad in a thin gray jumpsuit and disposable flipflops.

The healthy ones are run across the grounds to the training building for their first in-person meeting with me. Blindfolded and naked, I want to see if they can feel my presence. I look for reactive cocks and if I see one, the boy has a 50/50 chance. Pain sluts are easy to rent, so I test their pain level, usually with small percussion tools. Sucking dildoes tells me if they are competent enough to rent out to clients with that kink, a frequent request from my regulars. A camera on a flexible arm discloses any anal tearing, a quick way for an applicant to be put on a bus ride home.

The exceptional applicant who passes those tests is allowed to spend a night in a small cage in an Intake anteroom where he is monitored and fed. In the morning, Jack takes him to the stable dorm for a daily enema after the rest of my slaves are cleaned out, then he joins the first of three piss-and-shit lines on the daily schedule. He is always the last boy in line. He can bounce and groan but I do not tolerate leakers.

There is a lot more I want to know before I take in an applicant but only after a boy passes those tests will I even bother to show him a slave contract.

My process of evaluating applicants works well and has evolved over time. How much time or thought could these six women have invested in the process? They all checked the box on the Parlor interest form saying they wanted to offer applications. After all, it's less expensive to recruit online than to buy from top-notch sellers. The women were new at this, so they didn't have trusted contacts like mine. They had no idea which sellers were reputable and which were crooks.

How to find quality applicants was the next session of the Parlor.

-=o=-

The guests were editing the items for their slave contracts when I arrived. Six heads turned toward me and six mouths dropped open when they saw my pet dog, Aussie, on all fours at my side. Aussie was a gift from Maeve and Annalise's Femdom Pet Shoppe. He is my guard dog and is always with me when My Cop has to work remotely.

Aussie is a good dog. He is always on alert for possible trouble and is well-trained at dealing with it. When he arrived, My Cop kept him in his attic cell and never took his eye off him for two weeks. Aussie was a qualified security officer but My Cop schooled him in the finer techniques of protection, defense and defeating intruders, not just deactivating them. Totally and completely putting them out of commission to the point they faced a long-term recovery. When Aussie passed My Cop's strenuous tests, he was allowed to meet me.

I had a lovely collar made for him. It complements the tail that dangles from his ass. Because he is on all-fours all the time, the Pet Shoppe girls outfitted him with knee and paw pads when they delivered him. They're a nice touch.

I introduced them to Aussie. "Taking in applicants is risky," I said. "If you are not 100% convinced of a slave's loyalty, you want to have protection."

The women nodded. Being safe should always be on a Domme's mind.

"One of my exclusives is my primary defender. When he is remote, I have Aussie. Any lowlife who even thinks about invading my personal space will wind up in rehab."

The women shook their heads in admiration. I felt Aussie stiffen on his leash. He is proud of how well he guards me and keeps me safe. It's a good thing, too, because if he failed, My Cop would come down hard on him. Aussie has seen My Cop in action and his main fear, second only to my single-tail, is My Cop's fury. He's seen what it can do.

That reprobate is still undergoing physical therapy.

"Let's talk about applications," I said. "You asked my slaves questions so you should understand a lot more about what you want to know about boys who apply. An application must tell you what you every detail about a boy before you agree to talk to him, much less meet him in person."

Aussie growled.

"That's his way of agreeing with me. Meeting unknowns is fraught with danger."

The women picked up their pens. It was time to make a list.

CHAPTER 8

The Application

GROWING A STABLE means buying, trading for or accepting boys who apply. Fitting in the ones you buy from a trusted seller or through a trade with reputable vendors is time-consuming enough. When the boy is an applicant, the process is extra complicated. It takes more time for that kind of boy, one who's never been owned, to submit to your rules in real life. Then there is your time spent monitoring his progress. It is a sad fact but a fact nonetheless. Some of them will fail and you will have to get rid of them.

Dismissing an applicant who made it through an initial assessment is distasteful and worse, filled with hazards. I have heard of terminated slaves who try to attack the owners. Then there are sagas of rejected boys who stalk the Domme and her residence.

That's why well-written applications and contracts are crucial. This part of the Parlor would show the guests how to prevent problems.

If you have clients who are in law enforcement or even better, judges, then your problem may be resolved more easily. But if you are starting out and do not yet have tested methods in place or protection from upset rejects, you must make sure your application weeds out the problems before you reveal your name or location.

Get a dog. A trained guard dog.

After I told the six Parlor guests some of the more lurid stories about Dommes who were victimized by vengeful castoffs, they were eager to get to work on their own slave applications. Not one of them wanted to deal with stalkers or troublesome throwaways.

"A Domme should *never* be afraid of her slaves. They must be *committed* and *devoted* to you."

The women nodded. Aussie barked his agreement.

"You interviewed six of my slaves. Listen to your questions and their responses and be ready to tell me the best questions you should use on your application form."

They weren't surprised I recorded them. That did not stop them from being embarrassed about the poor quality of what they asked.

"First up is Martha and then Chevelle. Their questions pointed to the same answer from different slaves. Martha asked my #40, a pain slut and screamer who longs for my whip, about speaking freely to me. Listen."

I had my girl play Martha's question.

"What would you tell your owner if she let you speak freely?"

My boy answered.

"I am not free. I do not speak freely."

I let that sink in and moved to the next one. "Chevelle had #51, a big, beautiful dark-skinned slave whose cock and ass were tattooed with his number. The tattoos have an important meaning." Then I added, "I'm sure she noticed his 8.25" cock."

The girls giggled. They all noticed the extra-large cock cage imprisoning a shaft they wished was theirs. My girl played Chevelle's question.

"What is your biggest and most important two duties as a slave?"

#51 said,

Obedience. Fidelity.

They heard his words yet I wasn't sure they understood the implications of what he said were his most *important* duties. How would they work his reply into a question?

"Which of you is clever enough to turn those answers into questions for your application?"

Silence. They were thinking. Then Beatrix actually raised her hand. Dommes do not raise their hands. If she didn't look so serious, I would have laughed.

I nodded and she said, "Both of your slaves said things that told me they knew they were owned. And they more than just accepted it. It was like imprinted on them. In their minds. It wasn't only about their bodies."

Beatrix's comments were insightful even if they weren't sophisticated. As long as she got the point, I ignored her phrasing.

"Exactly. It's very easy to own and control a boy's body. It's much more insidious to own his mind."

They wrote feverishly on their papers.

"How would you say that in a question?" Simone asked.

Bingo! That is exactly what this part of the Parlor was designed to do. "Sometimes running ideas by like-minded women helps. Give it a try," I said.

Simone thought for a moment and said, "How about this? If I accept you as my slave, are you willing to obey every command I give you?"

I shook my head side-to-side. Slaves aren't *willing* to give me bupkis. I take it from them.

Martha tried rewording it. "Do you understand that my ownership of you is complete, your body and your thoughts. Failure to obey is punishable by expulsion. Answer yes or no."

That was more like it. Slaves should *never* be given the option to answer in sentences. Checkboxes are a better choice. There is no gray between yes and no.

"Excellent! Write that down and when you meet with your attorneys, explain why you are using forced-choice questions."

The guests were on their way massaging my slaves' answers into application questions. I wanted to see how they would use Beatrix's question to my #89, a boy I had only six months. He was my second video and audio editor. The one I bought in Memphis was working out well but I had more marketing ideas and needed a second one. I put in an order with Ned and in less than a week I had two video inspections. I chose the smaller one.

"The small ones eat less," Ned said. "They're cheaper to keep."

I had the girl play Beatrix's question.

"How does having your owner control everything you do every day, down to the last detail like when you can pee, make you feel?"

Of course, I would never have asked about how a boy feels, but #89 had a good answer. Just one word.

Comforting.

That was unsurprising because I knew his history. Many males cannot manage their own lives. They have trouble focusing on one goal and are too easily distracted by every shiny object they see. In my stable, there are no shiny objects, just rigorous schedules. That makes males focus and achieve the goal they are assigned. *Comforting* was the correct word for this boy.

"Who wants to offer a question that identifies applicants as typical males who need daily structure imposed on them?"

I was glad to see Chevelle raise her hand. At some point, I'd tell them that authentic Dommes do *not* raise their hands. Later. I was having too much fun imagining them as little school children. I nodded.

Chevelle said, "I would ask two questions on the form. First, do you have a daily schedule with what you have to finish at the top? And second, how often do you reach that goal?"

Spoken like a true factory worker who had to meet a daily quota. But it is a first-rate way of dealing with male slaves. With a little rewording, her question was a good way to tell typical males they had to achieve the required result. Chevelle's face lit up when I smiled.

"Outstanding! The only tweak I'd suggest is to list common daily goals. Many males have trouble articulating exactly what their goals are. We tell them what their results will be. We tell them what they will do and when it will be done. Like my #89 said, knowing he had to obey my rules comforted him."

They wrote more notes and Chevelle raised her hand again. This was getting too funny. My neck was getting tired of nodding.

"Men are stupid," she said. "They have to be told what to do."

Chevelle just earned an invitation to an upcoming Parlor. She had the right stuff. Like a seedling, she needed sunlight and water to grow.

"Let's hear Simone's question to #57. I've owned him for two years. He's an outdoor worker with a decent 7.25" cock. Unlike Chevelle's boy, it did not bear his number. Think about that."

The girl played the question.

"What did you give up to live as a slave?"

My boy replied without a moment's hesitation.

Everything.

"What does that tell you?" I asked, hoping someone would answer without raising her hand but Parker's was waving in the air.

"I think Simone should have asked what he gave up to be *your* slave. I don't want a boy who just wants to be *anyone's* slave. I want a boy who *has* to be mine — not *wants* to be. He *needs* to be *my* slave."

Aussie woofed in agreement. I was right about Parker. She had the makings of what it takes to join our network. Some day.

We talked for an hour and they bounced suggestions off each other. After the conversation, they had a list of questions that would give them what they had to know before taking in an applicant.

By the end of the hour, there were only two questions and answers left to play. I had my girl play Parker's first.

"I know your owner gives you the basics, like food and shelter. Aside from those, what is the most important thing your owner gives you?"

#34, a slave I've had for three years, is a role-player who is requested so often my girl can't schedule appointments for him for at least two months. He said,

Ms. Amity owns me, body and mind. It's the greatest gift.

I didn't have to ask. Three hands were waving wildly in the air. I was waiting for them to chant, "Pick me! Pick me!" Simone went first. Bossy Dommes like her don't wait to be called on.

"How in the heck do we ask a written question and know if the answer is sincere?"

I hesitated to tell her that is what experience means, so I let the others answer.

"I can pick out a liar," Chevelle said.

Parker added, "I could feel his honesty. That's why having him in person can be helpful."

Aussie growled. Parker quickly added, "With proper protection, of course."

I patted Aussie's bald head and said, "Good boy." He wagged the tail hanging out of his ass.

Martha was shifting in her chair, still raw from the pussy jolts she suffered earlier. She kept her hand high until I called on her. I wonder if she grasped that my prod taught her to obey and the lesson would be a constant reminder all day? She'd remember it tomorrow, too.

"A boy must be grateful for everything I give him. He may not complain if he doesn't get what he wants."

That is true but it wasn't a question for an application. Martha was halfway there. I pushed her to go all the way.

"Tell me your question," I said fingering the prod on my belt. She saw my left hand fondling the device and rushed to answer.

"What do you get out of slavery to me?"

So close. Inches away. I propelled Martha across the finish line.

"Try again," I said and pressed the prod's power button. She saw it light up and trembled. She was almost in tears.

"How about this? When you are my slave, what do I owe you and what do you owe me?"

The women could work with that and their lawyers would knead it into the legalese they love. But I was having too much fun toying with Martha. She was scared of the prod in my left hand. She should be. I knew she wasn't wearing panties and that made her pussy an easy target. Too easy.

There were three questions left, all from Danica. I had a feeling she knew there was more to my #99 than met her eye. If she did, if she sensed what was boiling inside him, I had plans for Danica.

Very big plans.

CHAPTER 9

DANICA'S INNER VOICE

"WHY DID YOU SIGN Ms. Amity's contract?" Danica's question played on the speakers. She was interrogating #99, a boy I owned — completely — for only a few weeks. With this boy, the number of weeks was unimportant. He gave himself to me two years ago but the timing wasn't ideal, not for him and not for me. I rarely wait for boys to submit to my ownership. This one was special.

There are precious few slaves I regard as special.

The Parlor guests had to learn what makes a slave special. They had to stand face-to-face with an authentic one to fully understand the phenomenon. There aren't many genuinely special ones out there, so when you find one, listen to your inner Domme voice. It will be shouting at you.

#99 didn't hesitate to answer her question. Special slaves have only one reply to a question like hers.

Because this is where I am supposed to be. Where I WANT to be!

Her follow up was superb. She went straight to the heart of slavery.

"Can Ms. Amity trust you?"

When I heard his answer, my inner voice was screaming.

I would die before I violated Ms. Amity's trust.

And finally, she asked the exact question I pose to my slaves. Twice. Once when they are uncrated in the transport garage and two weeks later when they complete Intake.

"Who are you?"

#99 shouted,

MS. AMITY OWNS ME!

When the replay finished, Aussie nudged my ankles. He felt it, too. Pure, honest passion.

I guess Aussie's inner doggie voice was barking at him, too.

Before I could ask if anyone knew how to translate that exchange into useful application questions, Danica stood up and took over the conversation. She didn't want any of the other women's input. She didn't need anything they had to say. She knew.

"Written questions, checkboxes, yes/no choices. They're all helpful." Danica took a deep breath. "None of them will reveal a slave's true hunger. His urge, his thirst for your ownership is intimate. It will radiate from his heart. No online form can tell you that."

I walked over to Danica, wrapped my arms around her and whispered, "You've met that slave. You own that slave."

She nodded into my shoulder and Aussie nudged her calves.

The other five Dommes sensibly kept their mouths shut. Had they tried to talk, I'm sure Aussie would have growled at them.

They now had a series of questions for their application forms. This was the perfect time to bring up video interviews.

Technical considerations came first. Make sure you see the slave and he cannot see you. Block your IP address, either through a VPN or other means. Install a hardware firewall. Use an anonymous video conferencing tool. In other words, hire a trusted IT consultant. The cost is an investment in your future.

Once we were clear on technology, technique was next.

The Parlor building is wired with monitors on all the walls. When the screens focused, a male's face appeared. He wasn't one of my slaves; instead, he was an actual applicant who made it through the first round of background checks. He thought he was talking only to me. Males who assume anything about me are usually wrong. Like this one.

I clicked my headset button, unmuted the mic and spoke to him. "Stand up. Strip."

The women watched him pause for a moment before obeying, a typical reaction for males like him. Unowned. Clueless.

After muting my microphone, I addressed the women.

"This boy is available and I have no use for him. One of you can have him if you earn him. I will choose the winner based on how proficient your interview techniques are."

Beatrix and Simone smiled evilly. Chevelle wore a broad grin. The idea of being gifted a slave that passed my initial application and background check was enticing. Parker looked nonchalant, like a free slave was an everyday occurrence. Martha was still shifting in her chair from what I knew would be a permanent pussy memory.

Danica didn't smile or frown. Her face was hard to read. Even though she needed to add to her stable if for no other reason than to tend to all the maintenance her new property required, she wasn't overly eager. That's a mark of a good owner.

I turned on my mic and spoke to the boy whose naked body now filled every monitor in the building.

"Turn around. Do not speak. Jiggle your ass up-and-down for yes, side-to-side for no. Do you understand?"

He spun and wiggled his ass vertically. That taught the women an important lesson. There is almost nothing a slave has to say that I want to hear. They speak when I give them permission. Which is rarely.

"You read the contract overview?" I asked. His wiggling ass confirmed it. "Hands up high." He complied. "Now touch your toes."

An experienced Domme would know where I was going. Judging from their faces, Simone and Chevelle couldn't figure it out but Beatrix leaned forward. Instead of wriggling in her chair, Martha used the opportunity to walk over to a wall monitor for a closer look. Parker wrote notes on her paper.

Danica moved next to me and whispered, "May I please have the microphone, Ms. Amity?"

I handed her my headset, pressed her finger on the mute button and stepped aside. Had she figured out the next step?

"Spread your cheeks," she said firmly.

The boy struggled to keep his balance but managed to obey her order. I'm sure she saw my smile when I waved my finger in a circle, telling her to continue.

"Put the plug on the chair and sit on it."

The other women stared at the screen until they, too, saw that the tools I require video interviewees to have handy. If the boy had prepared properly, his ass was already lubricated. If not, I would end the call. I have no need for stupid slaves.

The boy followed her order and let out a small groan when the plug was fully inside his ass. Danica ignored the noise.

"Bounce."

He sucked a little air and bounced. If he had a proper slave's mindset, he wouldn't stop until she told him to. He bobbed up and down while Danica watched. Her inner Domme voice was true.

While he bounced, Danica muted the mic and handed the headset back to me. I offered it to the audience and had an idea who would take it. Parker was game and thanked me for the chance.

"Stand and keep that plug inside."

The boy clamped his asscheeks and stood up. His cock and balls filled every monitor on the Parlor building's walls.

Parker said, "Ruler."

The boy picked up the ruler that was on his list and held it until Parker told him to press it against his shaft. Everyone saw the result. The hard cock measured almost eight inches. There was only one thing wrong.

It was hard.

My boys are not allowed to erect unless a hard shaft serves my purpose. I have them milked three times a week unless they misbehave. Then it's every day and sometimes twice. The milking machine can do twelve at a time, so it's easy to finish them in just a few minutes. Besides, after they finish Intake, they are caged. Cock cages keep the stable calm.

With the mic muted, I spoke to the onlookers. "Who wants to take care of it?"

If they didn't think an unordered erection was disobedient, their Domme voices weren't talking loudly enough and I had little hope for their future success.

I pointed at Simone, the Florida gal with the huge bosom and bossy attitude. Surely a Domme like her knew what to do.

Simone wasn't enthusiastic about being put on the spot, but I wasn't making a request. She fit the headset over her ears and before she said a word, I pinched her nipples. She was going to interview this boy despite what my fingers were doing to her. I had a reason and it was hers to decipher.

"Tell him what to do," I said.

Simone unmuted the mic and said, "Slap that cock."

The boy did. Once. I pinched harder.

"Again," she said.

Aussie nudged my foot. I looked down and he had a pair of nipple clips in his teeth, evidently delivered by one of my girls. They are so well trained, I seldom have ask for small things like the clamps in Aussie's mouth. After clipping Simone's huge bosom and tightening the teeth, she gave the boy another command.

"Slap with each hand." He did.

"Again," she said.

Simone was getting it, albeit slowly. Chevelle whispered loud enough for Simone to hear, "Harder."

If Simone's Domme voice wasn't talking to her, Chevelle's was happy to assist.

"Harder!" Simone finally said.

The boy did as he was told, grunting each time he slapped himself. If the boy had the capacity to be a useful slave, he would continue until he was ordered to stop.

Which is exactly what he did.

I took the headset a few minutes later and instructed him to stand at attention until I had time for him. He would do that because I had listened to his video statement about why he wanted to enter slavery. He might turn into a decent worker, but he had no place in my world. I don't take decent ones. I demand more than that, a lot more, before I'm even mildly interested. Besides, I knew who needed him and the price was right.

"Girls, let's have lunch and talk over that interview and what you learned."

As for the boy standing at attention somewhere in the continental United States, he would be on my monitor later if I remembered to dismiss him. Then I would award him to the winner.

AMITY HARRIS

CHAPTER 10

LUNCHEON

THE CHEF I BOUGHT in Memphis had trouble working in the same kitchen with the one I picked up in Sweden. They are both artists so I kept an eye on them because artistic types, no matter what their talents, are prone to emotional episodes. Unless you keep your finger on them, they turn into divas. There is no place for divas in my household.

The new one was relegated to being the sous chef, a subordinate role he wasn't used to and didn't like at all. A slave's expectations, no matter what skills he has, have no bearing on my decision where to place him. Only the quality of the meals they prepare sways me. What to do about it? That was the choice I was facing.

The Memphis chef often served tastier meals than the Swedish one. Ordinarily, I would switch their roles and if either acted up, a session with my single-tail would take care of it. Given the six Dommes around the dining room table, I saw the situation as a teachable moment for the chefs as well as for my guests.

The women would solve the problem. How they handled the two slaves would reveal a lot about how they would address their own stable conflicts. Shuffling slaves' responsibilities, especially with males, can disrupt a household's smooth functioning. They get testy. Or sad. Sad slaves are useless.

"Girls, I am sure you will enjoy lunch. We have a treat today. My two chefs have prepared different lunch menus. You will decide which tastes better. That gives you an opportunity to weigh in on which one I will appoint as head chef."

Smiles all around. For women like these, exercising power over slaves is almost better than whipped cream on blueberry pie. Almost.

I had the chefs' dishes served by the kitchen staff so the guests would not know which chef prepared each dish. While we tasted the options, we chatted about flavor and presentation. Even Aussie had two bowls on the floor in the corner but he was not given a vote. He eats well but not off the table.

We enjoyed a three-course meal, a salad, main course and dessert. Almost every plate was licked clean, especially Aussie's bowls. When dessert was served, Nova jogged in and waited for me to recognize her. With huge breasts and jiggling layers of fat, she was hard to miss.

I nodded at her and she nodded back. A delivery was being uncrated in my transport garage. I pointed to my feet and she knew what to do. She trotted out as silently as she entered, jiggling all the way.

"That's a well-trained female," Beatrix said. "Maybe I should get one of those."

I smiled. Beatrix does mostly paid work but wanted to grow her small stable of rentables. They would provide income when she was with a client. In my network, we call that a two-fer.

"I don't know how you can manage a household without your own female," Parker said. "I mean, who handles your clothes? Makeup? Hair?"

Chevelle thought a female was just an expense, a luxury. Martha agreed. Her focus is usually about cost.

"There are other choices for a personal slave," I said. "Ones that are rentable."

To say the least, they were surprised.

"What are those options?" Simone asked. "I mean, a personal female does, well, personal things. Who else could do those things?"

A kitchen slave added more whipped cream to my blueberry cobbler and I jolted Nova. She ran in and waited for me to acknowledge her.

"Get it," I said.

She ran out, jiggling with each step. In a few minutes, she returned with my newest eunuch behind her. I sent her away and had the gelding spin around to show my guests its new body.

"One of these," I said. "Not only are they easy to train, they often have a penchant for intimate things like wardrobe, hair and makeup, all the way to bathing. They are inexpensive to keep although creating them is costly. However, they are frequent rental requests."

Several of my guests' lower jaws dropped. I was pretty sure they'd heard of eunuchs but had never seen one before.

"How much do they cost?" Danica asked. Actually, they can be fairly cheap at an auction but then you are getting someone else's work.

"Don't buy one. Create your own. The trick is making sure you have the right boy before you start. And an excellent medical team."

"Ms. Amity, may I see it up close?"

Danica was fascinated with my new eunuch. She had dozens of questions and all of my attention. She patted where its penis and testicles used to hang and explored its tiny vagina I had built so it could pee without a tube. Its breasts were beginning to fill in and I keep it completely hairless.

"I could use one of these," Danica said after examining its body. I wasn't surprised. Once you see the benefits of having a sexless personal slave, you understand its potential profit. There are clients who request the gelding weekly and are thrilled to use it in the out-buildings I remodeled as cabins for longer-term rentals. I made a mental note to discuss the pros and cons of a eunuch with her later.

The guests were tasting and comparing the dessert offerings when I felt it. It's something I sense before I see or hear him. My Cop had arrived in transport, was run through Intake in record speed and was waiting outside the dining room. He would never enter without my direct order.

No one tells My Cop what to do except me.

The women at the table were involved with their chocolate mousse and key lime pie. They had no idea something special was just outside the door. Except Danica. I saw her look up, like she sensed something.

I jolted his chip. He crept in and settled under the table at my feet. That's his place. That's where he belongs.

I picked a few blueberries from my dessert and pressed them into his mouth. He was hungry but not for blueberries. His appetite was for my fingers. He sucked long and hard. I knew he was starving for what only I can feed him.

Most of my guests paid little attention to what they thought was just another slave under the table. Not Parker. Not Danica. They knew whoever the slave was under the table, he was different. Their inner Domme voices told them this one was unusual. Special. Exceptional.

The rest of them? They could be Dommes but they would hardly qualify for my network right now.

Danica and Parker shared another quality. They knew better than to ask about him. Instead, they watched me feed his hunger.

Simone blurted out, "What is that slave doing under the table?"

She was inches away from a return trip to the airport. She needed a lesson, a thorough one that she would remember for a long time. I had the perfect tool. It was slurping his bowl in the corner.

"Aussie! Fetch!" I called in his direction.

The dog dropped what he was chewing and scurried out of the room. Before I fed My Cop another fingerful of blueberries, Aussie was at my side, gripping a chain in his teeth. The new nipple clamps I ordered dangled from the ends of the chain. I use clamps on nipple slaves, the ones who scream crazily when their nipples are squeezed. These are much fiercer. Metal teeth. Adjustable tension. They don't fall off.

Simone's eyes opened wide when she saw the clips. I took them, patted Aussie's bald head and sent him back to the corner to finish his food. My Cop didn't flinch. If the clamps were going on his chest, he accepted that. Period. That's another reason he's My Cop.

I fingered the chain. Simone stopped eating. So did everyone else.

I pushed more blueberries into My Cop's mouth and stared at Simone. There are limits and this one was inviolable. No one interferes with my exclusives, especially Domme wannabees like Simone.

"The mousse is delicious!" Parker said, breaking the tense silence. "Can we have seconds or is that rude?"

Several women let out the breaths they were holding. There was some chatter about the lunch menu but I didn't hear a word of it.

Forks clinked against plates until Danica reminded everyone about rating the chef's presentations. "Shall we vote?"

My fingers relaxed a little. So did My Cop's grip on them. He has an inner voice, too. It talks to him and connects to me.

I dropped the clamps on the table as a reminder. "Fetch the chefs," I said and Aussie scooted to the kitchen. When he returned, my two chefs' cock cage rings were leashed together with the free end in Assie's teeth. They were clad only in pink frilly aprons.

"There is a lot riding on your votes. The menu with the most votes will be my new head chef. The loser? That one will be monitored and if he fails to please me? He gets put up for sale."

If the women were surprised, the two chefs were stunned. While they commented on each dish and I allowed the chefs to answer their questions, my fingers pushed blueberries into My Cop's mouth.

The way he sucks my fingers ignites the ever-present fire that smolders inside me and he turns it into an inferno. I would have him tonight and my night would not end till morning.

As for the applicant still standing at attention somewhere in the continental United States, I gave him to Chevelle. She used him for the hour off after lunch before we returned to the Parlor to test him. I'd call Red Rick later to ship him to Texas. As for the applicant, he would be happy that he had an owner.

He better be. My single-tail has a long reach.

Remote Slaves

CHAPTER 11

REMOTE SLAVERY

NOT EVERY DOMME can keep slaves where she lives. Some are in cities and don't have acres of land. Even those of us who have space don't always want to deal with an in-house stable. Not only is it a lot of work, it's expensive. Perhaps over time you can collect enough rentable boys to meet your costs, but it's still a huge undertaking.

That's where remote slaves come in. Some have skills you need but not long term. You need what they can do but they may not be frequent rentals, so having them at your disposal remotely is an efficient way to keep them. Of course, you need to monitor and control them and set up a schedule to use them. I do not tell my remotes when they will drop what they're doing to perform a task I need done. Surprising them keeps them in line.

Random use keeps them on their toes. My remotes fill out calendars so I know where they are and can drop in unexpectedly. Once the video and audio is installed in their homes and most workplaces, my girls check on them routinely. When I want one, whether to do a task or just to remind him of my ownership, my remotes make themselves available. Immediately.

For the past two years, that's how #99 lived. He needed that time to finish his service before putting in his papers. But I could see him when he was at home and spoke to him almost every night. Keeping him on a tight schedule and a tighter leash kept him on an even keel.

My Cop is different. The work he does makes overseeing him a challenge, what with his security detail and the clandestine places he goes. My girls have no access to him. He is all mine.

The advantage of remote slaves is they are overwhelmingly applicants. You choose what skill you want and have them delivered to you for a few weeks so they learn to obey your rules. Weeding out the pretenders is much easier when they're standing naked in front of you. If a boy acts up or doesn't fit in, it's stress-free to ship him home and never have to see him again. That's why I recommend hiring a quality research team. They can strip cameras out of a dismissed slave's home when he's at the grocery store. The best part is you never have to worry about stalkers or the ones who can't cope with rejection.

But when I need a remote to do a job? They're close to perfect.

The Parlor afternoon covered remote slaves. How to find them. How to control them. How to use them.

The women gathered in the Parlor building after lunch and an hour of free time. My girls kept an eye on them, a video eye, and if they didn't know they were being observed, they should have. Did they think I would allow women I don't yet trust to have free reign in my world?

Chevelle spent the hour in a small room off the main Parlor area working her new slave and observing him from every angle. Martha soaked in a jetted tub in the bathroom attached to the bedroom she shared with Beatrix. Martha would remember my prod between her legs every time she sat on a chair. I presumed she would take that lesson and use it on her property. It works particularly well with females.

I put Beatrix and Martha together when I saw how avidly Beatrix sucked Martha's nipples during our morning session. Later that night, my girls would tell me if they took that experience to a more intimate place. There were several ways Beatrix could alleviate Martha's pussy pain and I was curious which she would choose.

Simone shared a room with Chevelle, so Simone had it to herself for the after-lunch hour. Her nipples were still sore and my girls noted how she stripped and masturbated for the entire hour. That told me volumes about her. She wasn't nervous that I would clamp her again. In fact, she hoped I would. If Simone had been a slave instead of a Domme, she would make a rentable pain slut.

Parker and Danica shared a suite. They had more in common with each other than they did with any of the other women. Danica already knew a lot that Parker could learn, especially since she inherited that big house and planned to rent space to her clients to use her boys. Both of them were in growth stages. Their goals were similar. They wanted more slaves, more clients to rent them and more income to pay for their new lifestyles. I wanted them to turn into butterflies.

When the hour was over, we had work to do.

The Parlor building was set up and several of my remotes were jolted — implanting their chips was done during their two-week stay in the stable dorm — and were ready for whatever I assigned. The women saw them on the monitors and with their faces masked, would never know who they were or where they lived. My remotes are valuable and I hardly ever share them.

They settled into a circle of chairs, facing out so they could see all the monitors. I walked around the outside of the circle and pointed out various considerations about remote slaves.

"You know that remote slaves are cheaper. They almost never interrupt your schedule. It's easy to get rid of one if he's a problem. Those are the positives."

The women nodded. Nothing I said was surprising.

"However, finding one, a really good one, is actually more difficult than buying one. Who can tell me why?"

I predicted one of them would raise her hand. This time, it was Beatrix.

"I imagine there are a lot who want to be used only occasionally."

Parker added, "Those aren't slave material."

They all had derisive comments about that kind of male. Apparently they were experienced with the "Me! Me! Me!" ones. Those are the ones who beg for a spanking and then complain about how much it hurts.

"That makes finding the right males to be your remotes difficult. You need a method, a way to know if he is something you want to invest your time in. More than that, you have to be sure that when you assign him a task, he will do it. Do it well. Do it now."

Dommes-for-hire are experts at phone sex and nowadays, video sex. Men ooze the need to be dominated and some women are very good at that, usually for money. I have no problem with them or what they do. As long as it's safe, sane, consensual and adult, grown-ups should have fun.

But that's not what the six women in my Parlor were after.

"Look at the males on the monitors," I said. "See their posture? They are at full attention, waiting. They will remain like that until I tell them what to do. Who can tell me why they are so obedient?"

I tried not to laugh when Martha raised her hand but it was becoming harder and harder to hide my amusement. I nodded at her and she said, "Because they're trained?"

It was a question, not an answer. I moved to the next hand in the air and Chevelle said, "Because they will be punished if they disobey."

At least that was a statement, not a question. My expectations for Chevelle rose a notch.

"That's a big part of it," I said. "But it's not all of it. Who knows what the other, bigger part is?"

They thought for a while and I almost lost hope any of them would be able to articulate it. The problem was they were thinking about today. Today is not your main focus. There will always be a tomorrow. The future is what you should be planning for.

"They are frightened to death that you will dismiss them. They want to serve you with their hearts, not only their bodies."

"Exactly!" I said. Danica almost smiled while the others frowned. Danica knows a slave's heart. The scowling women had never stood face-to-face with a male who was totally committed to her, body and mind. Until you feel that passion, that need, you can be a Domme, but you will never be an authentic one. I almost felt sorry for them. Almost.

I passed out pre-printed cards and told the women to read what was on theirs, then match the number to a monitor. "You will give the boy the orders and the time limits on your cards. Use your own words and your own tone of voice. Each boy is capable of completing the job in the time allotted. We will evaluate your success or failure when the time is up."

One of my girls handed out headsets, each connected to their assigned boy's speaker. The women had their instructions. I was curious to see which of them would achieve the rather simple goal.

"Go!" I said.

Beatrix, Martha and Chevelle walked to the monitor that matched their boy's number and barked out commands. Those remotes ran to their computers to do the work. It wasn't complicated and each boy was given a job well within his expertise.

On the far wall, Simone stood near the monitor and gave her boy instructions. Twice. I think the names of the software she had to read were unfamiliar to her. Her boy wrote excellent marketing copy. It should be straightforward for him to write a 30-second blurb about the new nipple clamps. Simone was intimately familiar with them.

Parker stood up to give her orders to the boy assigned to her. She didn't walk over to the monitor but stared at it and the boy on the screen. When she was done, the boy moved to his chair and began the work she detailed.

Danica was last. She didn't stand up. She never looked at the monitor. She spoke calmly and I saw the boy wag his ass, the way my boys say yes. He ran in place, then bent over and spread his asscheeks. He didn't sit down to work until she was done breaking him in. To her.

I wasn't surprised at all when Danica's boy was the first to finish.

My girl muted Danica's mic and engaged mine. I had a few words for the boy and told him to expect a drop-in visit later that evening. While he waited, I set his chip to vibrate and jolt him at random times. Watching him wiggle in his chair and grunt was amusing. I smiled at Danica and she actually returned my grin.

"Time!" I called to the others. I took over their microphones and ordered the boys to stop work and pressed a button on my controller.

"What the hell are they doing?" Martha asked.

Simone's fingers crept under her bustier. They were working on her nipples. Hard.

"They failed to finish on time. That means *you* failed to get the job done. Each of my remotes is chipped. I have them implanted when I put them through Intake. Like I tell them, you won't like what happens to the ones who fail."

"I want me some of those chips!" Chevelle said.

Beatrix had a question. "I wonder what they feel like."

"Aussie, fetch!" I said and my dog scooted toward the girl I indicated. He pushed her toward me, his nose pressing against the back of her legs. I turned to Beatrix and said, "This is how it feels."

The girl fell on the floor, thrashed and screeched for a few seconds. When I changed the setting, she rolled into a ball and moaned from the pleasure mode. Then she writhed and screamed again.

"*That's* how it feels," I said. "Emma can implant one in you, if you'd like a more personal experience with my chip."

Beatrix's face turned red and she shook her head. Chevelle snorted and the other women laughed.

"What did you learn from that experiment?" I asked all of them but hoped Danica would be the one who answered. Her inner voice told her how to handle remotes and there was a lot the other women could learn from her. Was she confident enough to tell them what they did wrong? If she couldn't rise to that challenge, all her slave's money in the world wouldn't make her the Domme she was born to be.

No one raised their hands. Thank goodness.

Finally, Danica said, "You all told them what to do. But Ms. Amity owns them."

So close. So very close.

Then she added, "I took ownership first."

Touché!

We had one more exercise before dinner. I hoped Danica survived it.

CHAPTER 12

OWNERSHIP

DANICA'S SLAVE WAS locked in a small cell in the attic next to My Cop, two doors down from Zayn. I kept him away from the stable, isolated upstairs with my exclusives until I wanted to use them. That time was now, so I jolted Nova to retrieve them. They trotted behind her through hallways and down two staircases, then across the grounds to the Parlor building. The only one panting for air when they arrived was my female.

Nova needed more exercise so I had her trot to the slave dorm to bring the other one I wanted to use in this demonstration. A few minutes later, #99 ran in behind her and joined the others.

Nova was exhausted. I pointed to the door and she huffed and puffed her way out.

The four boys wore masks. That's my policy for my exclusives when they are among strangers. I thought it was polite to cover the boy Danica brought as well.

Earlier that day, I had Zayn spend time with Danica's boy. During the hour off after lunch, Zayn met with him and told me her boy was genuine. He knew it, he said, the moment he touched his chest and confirmed it when the boy shivered from a small charge they shared when their fingertips met. My Cop had already run a background check on him before I allowed him into my world.

What the Parlor guests saw was a line of four authentic slaves. Three were mine, two wore my brand. The third needed more time to prove himself, but I could visualize my initial broiled on his sac. Danica's boy had no permanent mark but I had a feeling that would change soon.

This was the final Parlor session and I intended it to show the six women how authentic ownership plays out in real life. Oh, they can talk about it and think they know what it is, but until they feel it, they will never understand what a sincere, true slave is. It's not something that can be explained with words. It's much bigger — and deeper — than words can do justice.

Lucky women will find that slave, the one who gives himself completely, utterly, absolutely to his owner. Slaves like that are rare and can show up in the most unlikely situations. You have to be open to finding one and when you do, your inner voice won't just talk to you. It will scream.

Only the most receptive women — authentic Dommes — hear that voice.

"Girls, take a close look at these four males. Walk around them but *do not* touch. When you finish, you are going to tell me what you sense about them and why you think I put these four on display."

I tapped Danica's arm to keep her at my side. She didn't have to take a closer look to know what an authentic slave was. Zayn looked at Danica and nodded at me. He felt it, too. She listened to her voice.

The women walked in front of the four naked males, behind them, between them and then took a last stroll down the line. Their jaws were tight from how hard they were focusing on the task I gave them. Beatrix took two tours behind them and checked their asses. Simone eyed them up and down repeatedly. Martha looked like she was evaluating their worth as if I were going to ask her how much she would pay for them. Chevelle wasn't sure what she was looking at other than four excellent examples of male flesh.

Parker approached Zayn and looked at me in surprise. I knew what her look meant when Zayn closed his eyes and sucked in in slow, even breaths. He felt her inner voice.

Danica kept an eye on each woman when they neared her slave. That's one reason I forbid them from touching. Danica wasn't ready for anyone else to handle her boy. Later tonight, she would learn how to regard him differently. And how to trust him. And me.

When the women were seated, I asked each to answer my original question, why I brought these four boys to the Parlor. I let them talk.

Simone said, "They look well trained and in very good shape. They must be examples of why we should keep our stables physically fit."

It was hard not to smile, but I kept mine in check.

"They must be very good at something," Beatrix said. "You're showing them off because they have special skills that pay well when you rent them."

I struggled not to smirk and pointed at Chevelle for her take.

"I bet you are going to sell them all. They would all go for pretty high prices."

I bent a little, pretending to adjust my boot so she wouldn't see my grin or Danica's tight smile. Chevelle's comment was stupid and Danica knew it. It was Martha's turn.

"They are probably ones you took in from other Dommes to break and train, you know, for pay. They look like they just had a session with a single-tail."

That was unsurprising. Money and whips are always the first thing on Martha's mind.

"I'm not sure, but there's something different about that one," Parker said pointing at Zayn. "And the one over there," she indicated My Cop, "he felt warm. Not like heat. More like a warmth. But that one," her chin tilted toward #99, "he doesn't belong with them."

I broke my silence when she made that comment about #99. "Tell me why you think he doesn't belong with the others."

Parker seemed at a loss for words but said, "He's not ... whole."

After Danica's return visit, I wanted to spend some time with Parker. She needed a few months to get her new mansion ready for rentals and be a little farther along adding rentables to her collection.

Six women. After a full day of Parlor exercises, I had hope for two of them. I wanted to send the other four to transport take them to the airport. Heck, I just wanted them out of my sight. They'd be gone in an hour anyway but that meant I had to endure 60 more minutes of those clueless women.

"Parker, stand next to Danica."

When she was in place, albeit a little startled at being singled out, I spoke to the four seated women. The leftovers.

"There is a lot to know, tons to do, lists to make, tasks to finish before you should even consider bringing more slaves into your stable. Today you learned how much you don't know. My recommendation is that you discuss your experience with each other before any of you buys even one boy."

My brutal assessment dumbfounded them. Martha looked annoyed and Chevelle was crestfallen. Beatrix tried to keep a stiff upper lip but I predicted she would be a real Domme's personal female in less than a year. Simone's fingers were working their way under her bustier. That's apparently how she comforted herself.

"What about *them*?" Simone demanded. She was talking about Danica and Parker who were standing next to me.

"They are authentic," I said matter-of-factly.

"What the hell are we?" she asked. I heard the outrage in her voice. She was incapable of hiding it, a real weakness in a powerful woman.

"You are at the beginning of your journeys," I said. "You have a long way to go. I encourage you to take that time, figure out what your goals are and take the steps — one at a time — to reach them."

I was tired of explaining how incapable they were of running successful households and owning a stable. I'd keep tabs on Chevelle, but for now, I was done. I promised them a Parlor to teach them how to choose slaves and grow their holdings. I never guaranteed they would leave as reputable, respected Dommes who might one day join my network. Heck, they were lucky I didn't blackball them with my friends.

That was still a possibility. If I spread the word, they would never be able to buy from or sell to anyone I know.

"You will be leaving soon. Watch and learn."

It was getting late and the two chefs were busy preparing dinner for three. My hunger wasn't for food. I planned to summon My Cop after we ate so I'd have a night that wouldn't stop until the sun rose. Zayn was scheduled to work with #99 to help him reach his balance now that I owned all of him. These women were in my way.

I took Danica's arm and had her stand three feet away from her slave with Zayn between them. He touched their foreheads, one hand on each, and Danica twitched. Her slave shuddered.

His hand slid down their faces to their chins and worked slowly toward their chests. The boy trembled. Danica winced. Zayn's hands moved lower and the boy's eyes filled with tears.

Danica smiled. The biggest smile I'd ever seen on her face.

Zayn opened his eyes inched closer to me. He needs to be near me. That's where he regains his center when he guides others. It takes everything he is to act as the conduit between them and that often depletes him. My power restores his balance. I felt his need. It feels warm. Right then, I felt his whole heart.

The room was silent until Parker said, "Thank you, Ms. Amity. That was a privilege to watch."

"WHAT? What happened? What did they do?" Simone's tone was beyond challenging. It was ugly.

Not. In. My. World.

I had enough of her. I felt my anger rise when I told her what an uncouth boor she was.

"Get that bitch OUT of here!"

My Cop rushed toward me and Zayn leapt behind me, one to protect me and the other to absorb my fury. I don't get angry often but that woman's rudeness was outrageous.

#99 was eyeing My Cop, primed for his cue. Aussie jumped into action. He sprinted toward Simone and dragged her by her boot to the door. I didn't care where she ended up as long as it was hundreds of miles away from Amityworld.

Zayn laid his forehead on my shoulder. I felt a sort of calm flow into me. My Cop was crouched at my feet, almost daring the three seated women to say or do anything threatening. #99 bobbed up and down on his toes, ready to back up My Cop.

There was one thing left to do before this Parlor was officially over. This time, I didn't have to be the one who told them what they should have known.

"Tell them, Danica. Tell them how these four are different."

Still wearing that beautiful smile, Danica said, "You can have property. But you can truly, authentically own *only* those hearts and minds that are surrendered to you. Completely. Absolutely."

My two exclusives followed me out of the Parlor building and My Cop pointed at #99 to walk behind him. I jolted Nova and instructed her to get the three women packed and on their way to the airport. My house manager was told to move Parker to her own suite and have Danica's boy caged in hers.

Dinner was in an hour and I was hungry.

Dinner

CHAPTER 13

HUNGER

DINNER WAS ENTERTAINING with Parker and Danica in my smaller, more intimate dining room. My Cop was in his place under the table and Danica's boy was learning to do the same at her feet. Rather than leave Parker out, I had #99 on his knees near her. She was leaving in the morning and she was a charming addition to the table.

Zayn was in his attic cell, readying his oils and herbs for what I intended to be a very long night. Why have only one exclusive serve you when you can have two?

The two chefs were engaged in an awe-inspiring competition. My house manager reported they spent every minute after lunch preparing the courses they would serve for dinner. They knew the stakes and neither wanted to be relegated to second place or worse, being sold. After four courses and wine selected for each, we were treated to an array of desserts. I love choices so I chose to taste of them all. With whipped cream.

During dinner, I fed My Cop bits off my plate. He was ravenous for more than food. When I put my fingers in his mouth, he sucked each one and was disappointed whenever I pulled my fingers out. Danica and Parker followed my lead and we all agreed that having our fingers attended to like that was surprisingly sensual.

That was one reason I gave #99 to Parker to use during dinner. And why I moved her to a private suite.

Aussie enjoyed his dinner. His tail wagged when he cleaned his bowl with his tongue in the corner. When he was done, he curled up next to my chair and took a nap.

Our conversation touched on numerous topics. We explored some more deeply than others. Parker and Danica were eager to start renting slaves. The importance of owning boys who take care of your household and business and have a second rentable skill was new to them. They had heard about multi-talented slaves but wanted to know a lot more about how it worked.

I shared my system of examining for-sale merchandise and how important it is to know and trust the seller. The better sellers, the only ones I buy from, won't show me a boy who doesn't have that crucial second talent I can dangle in front of my clients. We shared some of the typical fetishes men have and laughed at many of them.

Parker started it off with, "Things they want in their asses! Cucumbers, dildoes, red nail polished fingers, on their knees, across my lap, at my feet! They are so detailed. When I give them what they've dreamt about for years you know what they do? They cry!"

It was good to see Danica laugh out loud at Parker's comments. I asked Danica to share some of the most unusual requests she had been asked to provide. Before answering, she filled her finger with caramel sauce and fed the boy at her feet. Her smile changed. It got wider when her boy sucked her finger clean.

"I was putting together a list of talents I need to buy," Danica said. "So many men try to hide what they really want. It's like what I learned about my boy. He needs my whip every morning like I need coffee."

I knew Danica didn't have a stable yet but she certainly had the place to put them. During the month her slave spent with me when she thought he was away on business,, I went through his plans and the architects' spec sheets. I suggested several modifications and additions and brought in Mason, the head of the construction crew I use that I often rent to Dommes in my network. He did a fine job at the Pet Shoppe and his reward was to be staked out in the field while the Shoppe owners sicced their trained dogs on him. Every time he sees Aussie, Mason gets a little tense.

Once my space planner's suggestions were worked into his plans, Danica's slave was assigned a cot in the slave dorm to learn how I house my boys. I had Jack deliver him to my office in the morning and had him explain everything he experienced in the dorm and how it impacted the plans. He was allowed to email his team, although my girls screened everything he sent.

One morning he said, "You showed me how important it is for My Owner to control every physical function."

I could almost hear the capital letters in his voice.

Two weeks in, the plans were finalized and the boy turned into one more slave in my stable. That meant he was rentable. My new marketing slave I bought in Memphis created a 30-second video and voiceover to show off Danica's boy's second skill. I knew he had it the moment I saw him but Danica didn't. Not yet. She sensed his need for her whip every morning but hadn't felt his other driving need. She would very soon.

Dinner was the perfect place to reveal it to her.

Over dessert I said, "I keep my exclusives in the attic. No one touches them except me. I don't rent them out. They are my personal property. I have to feel their sincerity, their indisputable need for my ownership before I buy or find them. That's how I got the two I have now."

Danica put her spoon down and looked at me. "My boy is my exclusive, isn't he?"

I nodded. She knew what he was. I just gave her the name for a unique slave like him.

"What is his other talent? What else can he do for you?"

She stared at her plate and picked at the whipped cream. "How do I find that out?"

I wish there was a quick answer to a question like that. There isn't but there are some ways to expose it. Of course, it would be a lot faster if I simply showed it to her.

If I have a boy for two weeks, you can be sure I know what he craves, what he will do anything to get. If that pleases you, then you found his elusive second skill.

I pressed a button and her boy screamed under the table.

Danica dropped her fork and Parker gripped the edge of the table. "What the hell was that?" Parker asked.

I smiled at both of them. "Get used to screaming slaves," I said. "Danica, drag his head between your legs."

When she touched his bald head, she finally realized it was *her* boy screeching in pain. She reached under the table and pulled his face between her thighs. In seconds, she stopped smiling, closed her eyes and leaned back in the chair. Parker gaped at her. I grinned. I gave her 30 seconds.

It only took 15 before she groaned. Loudly.

A few minutes later, Danica asked how I knew when she didn't.

"It doesn't matter how long you own a boy, especially an exclusive. There is always more mystery about him to unravel. Your boy? I had him implanted when I sensed his hunger to be controlled. A cage and a whip are one thing. A 24/7 microchip is better. And faster."

I handed her the control connected to her boy's chip. She fingered the buttons and pressed the yellow one. The boy screamed again but this time his face was already under her skirt and he lapped like a trained puppy.

"Oh my god, this is fantastic!" Danica said and closed her eyes again. While she enjoyed his tongue, I turned to Parker.

"The loaner at your feet? He gave himself completely to me a few weeks ago. He needs a lot of work and I've identified at least two unusual skills that I will grow so he is worthy of serving me exclusively. Would you like to have him for the night to see if you can detect the third?"

She didn't have to think about it and nodded repeatedly. "Thank you, Ms. Amity. That's very generous."

"When you discover the third one, be on the lookout for a fourth."

"Is he chipped?" she asked.

"Not yet. But if you can find the third and fourth, I'll have him implanted in the morning before you leave. Would you like to watch?"

Danica kept moaning. Parker beamed.

My night lasted until the sun rose. Neither Parker, Danica nor I got much sleep. The coffee I had delivered to our suites the next morning never tasted so good.

CHAPTER 14

BREAKFAST

WHEN BREAKFAST WAS served, Parker was so hungry she asked for seconds. Danica showed off the stripes on her slave's ass and she sat gingerly on her chair. My Cop was wrapped around my ankles, too exhausted to eat. The three of us had used them well. I wanted to hear about their nights.

Danica went first.

"Oh, Ms. Amity, you were spot on right! One little jolt to his chip and he pleaded to please me. Everywhere. He worked for an hour and when I was on my edge, I made him back off. I wanted more of it. I couldn't get enough."

"That's a critical quality of an exclusive," I said. "They should live to please you whenever and however you want. The good ones don't get tired because the only thing they want — the thing they *have* to do — is satisfy you. When you buy additional merchandise, make sure the skill you're paying for is so ingrained in their psyches that you can rent them by the hour for or a whole night."

Danica nodded and I sensed she was manipulating numbers in her head. Then I added a reminder. "I never rent my exclusives. What they do, what I keep them for, is entirely mine."

I wanted to know about Parker's night and hoped it was as enjoyable as Danica's. It's only been a few weeks that #99 has been in my absolute control and I had plans for him. Giving him to Parker for an evening was the first step in those plans.

"How did he do for you?" I asked.

She didn't need any encouragement. Parker was effusive. "Damn, he went all night! No matter what I wanted and even some things I didn't know I wanted, he gave me. In fact, it was like he knew what drove me to finish. Time after time."

"That's a quality I look for in a boy. Most males have native instincts but suppress them to satisfy their own desires. Sex turns into what *you* can do for *them*. Not for slaves with true hearts. I buy them if I sense they were born to serve me."

Parker kept nodding while I explained what else I look for in a potential exclusive.

"Ms. Amity, I can't remember the last time I came five times in one night! I'm not sure I ever did."

Danica moaned again. I let her have her fun and kept chatting with Parker. Then I asked the question she knew was coming.

"Can you tell me what his third skill is?" I asked.

"That's easy. The boy does *not* have a single skill. He is a package. He needs unwrapping."

That was as good a description of #99 as I could have come up with. When My Cop wanted to send him to me, he alluded to some of his history, but not the worst parts. When I had #99 here, I made him tell me each awful detail. Every one of them. How he was hiding his suffering the after-effects of his captivity. What they did to him was brutal. Inexcusable. Unfathomable. Anyone who survives that much torture truly deserves the life he wants.

#99 would never be a one-trick slave. He was a symphony of talents and when he was trained properly, he had the makings of an exclusive. Maybe even one of my own.

"Tell me what you learned about him," I said.

Parker thought for a moment and launched into a list. "You know he's strong and can go all night but you could say that about a lot of males. There is this insight he has, he kind of knows when I'm close and has the sense to back off. When he comes back, it's more intense than ever."

That was a good takeaway. I had one of my bare feet under the table on #99's ass. He felt calm.

"What else?" I asked.

"His hands. Well, really, his fingers. They are incredibly sensitive. I mean, when I let him suck my toes, he held each toe in his fingers and massaged it so … so … I don't know a word for how it felt. It was like a magic touch."

Parker knew two of his skills. #99's ass was still relaxed even though we were dissecting him and he could hear everything we said.

"Did you find the third?"

"That one? It took a while but I think it's in his ass. Not what goes in it. He's not one of the typical males who wants this or that thing stuffed inside. No, he has amazing reactions to hands on his cheeks. My hands. And he responds when I held on hard."

Parker needed a little encouragement to finish her thought. She also had to learn that we do not couch words when we talk about slaves. Part of our power is in how we name things, whether it's a boy or a technique. That's why I number mine. Stripping away their names equalizes them. So does shaving their heads.

But Parker was referring to something more than spanking and less than whipping. She had to give it a name. Only then could she own it.

"Hand? Ass? Be specific," I said.

"That's just it, Ms. Amity. I'm not sure what to call it but I damn sure know what to call how he reacted. Can you help me give it a name?"

Of course I could help. I own #99, from his body to his thoughts all the way to his reactivity. Heck, I practically built him. But Parker would never truly own a boy if she couldn't name him. I used my half-sentence tool to help her find the answer herself.

"When you slap his ass, he ..."

"When I slap his ass, he asks for more. Not more of the same. Different."

I tried again. "When you slap his ass, he wants you to ..."

"When I slap his ass, he wants ... no, he *needs* me to let his amazing fingers stimulate my pussy in ways I've never felt before. It's like he can make all his energy — and he's got a ton of it — flow into me. With just a touch. It's hard to describe."

No, it wasn't hard to describe. Parker was very close. She simply didn't have the right word but she darned well knew how it felt. His skill was always there, but it took hours of Zayn's magic to help #99 understand it. There is only one way to realize what Zayn's Tantric talents can unveil. You have to feel it and before you can feel it, you have to open yourself and let someone in. It took #99 several days before he would let Zayn's spirit inside him. It wasn't hard for me to know why it took so long.

I've seen Zayn take on others' pain and help them find balance. When he does, it drains him. Zayn's an emotional sponge. He absorbs their bad memories and forces them to float away. But for a time, he overflows with their sadness and grief. That's why his mentor, his guide, the old Asian Master I hired to tutor him, had Zayn share his essence with me. I hold his spirit and when Zayn becomes the conduit to release others' troubles, I keep him close.

It's beyond traditional Tantric ways. It's what connects me to Zayn. It's one of many reasons I made him my exclusive.

"Actually, that was a pretty good description," I said to Parker. "For now, let's call it #99's magic touch. Does that sound right to you?"

"Perfect," Parker said.

I kicked off my other shoe and pressed my foot on #99's asscheeks. He was a little tense, much as I expected. Two women were analyzing how his ass reacted to being spanked and he was naked under their feet. No wonder he was uneasy.

My other foot was in My Cop's mouth. After weeks of practice, he was now a first-class toe worshipper. It went well with breakfast.

I wanted Parker to name the fourth proficiency #99 had. If she was going to have a successful rental business, she had to recognize and buy slaves with specific aptitudes.

"The fourth skill? Did you find it?"

"You know, I think I may have found it. It has to do with his submission, doesn't it? How desperate he is to submit?"

Bingo! I liked Parker even more. She listens to the little voice inside her.

#99 was in physically severe shape when My Cop's team pulled him out. A lot of people died that day, most were his torturers. His recovery was complicated and even though his body healed and his spirit never wavered, it wasn't until My Cop pleaded for me to meet with the one he called 'the soldier' that he was finally able to heal from the damage the psychological part inflicted. The memories that tortured him. The one he couldn't bring himself to say out loud.

The evil he endured made him impotent. For years.

What Parker saw is what I sensed when I helped My Cop's soldier overcome the effects of that brutality. #99 never submitted to his captors. They hurt his body but he refused to let them into his mind.

I owned that now. I had to be sure he was giving himself to me freely, consciously, knowingly and willfully. That's why it took two years and two weeks before I let him in.

It's why I enforce a strict rule. There is no pain without a purpose.

Parker could not understand how enormous her comment was. Until #99 trusted me completely he would never trust anyone I gave him to. Last night, he didn't submit to her.

He submitted to me. To my ownership.

He trusted that I would make sure he was safe. If he was on his knees in in front of Parker, it was because he knew I was protecting him. Whips? Crops? Paddles? Those were small potatoes. He'd been through a lot worse than hell. Submitting to Parker was how he accepted and treasured my ownership.

Owning most slaves is simple. The special ones? They require more work. But they're worth every minute of your time.

CHAPTER 15

CHIPPING

DANICA PROBABLY NEVER enjoyed breakfast as much as she did that morning. The food was delicious and the coffee endless, but at least three orgasms later, Parker noticed the time and had only an hour before she left for the small airport to meet the plane that would take her home. I jolted Danica's boy and told her to bring him up for air.

"Aussie, fetch!" I said and my dog grabbed her slave's cock in his teeth and dragged him to my side. Then Aussie pulled My Cop from under the table and put him on the other side of my chair. When I make a decision, I don't wait. #99 proved himself to me last night with Parker and confirmed what I felt.

He was a keeper.

A couple of jolts later, the small dining room turned into a hub of activity. I had the kitchen girls clear the table and lay a sheet of plastic on top. Emma ran in with her kit and Nova delivered a small silver box from my office. The two slaves kneeling next to me had seen a box like that before. It held their microchips right before I had them implanted. In them.

Danica's slave stared at the silver box. My Cop nodded almost imperceptibly. Danica and Parker wore quizzical looks. As Emma unpacked her instruments, I pushed my chair back, reached under the table for #99's uncaged cock and used it to pull him to my feet.

"Who are you?" I asked him.

"MS. AMITY OWNS ME!" he roared. That's the only answer my slaves will ever give to that question.

"Put him on the table," I said and My Cop and Danica's boy hauled him into position, one they knew well. They laid him on his back and each pulled one of his ankles to spread his legs as far apart as they could go. Emma drizzled antiseptic under his testicles and waited for my go-ahead.

Before she started, I had something to say to my new permanent slave.

"I will keep you," I said. "Tell me what you want."

He didn't miss a beat. "Please, PLEASE, Ms. Amity! Keep me forever!"

"I own you. All of you. You are in my hands and I will keep you safe."

I nodded at Emma. She cut a half-inch slit in his perineum and pressed the chip inside. Then she applied the fast-acting glue my pharmacist developed that took less than an hour to seal the incision shut. I patted his perineum and had My Cop and Danica's boy put #99 on his feet.

His cock and balls were still in my hand. Nova handed me a temporary cage and I pulled his organs through the ring. They fit neatly into the device that would keep him erection-free for as long as I chose. When I clicked it shut, tears streamed down his face. He'd get his forever cage soon.

My Cop hugged his soldier and smiled when he returned to his place by my chair.

Danica and Parker thanked me for letting them witness a chipping. One of my girls carried Parker's luggage to the transport garage and we had a lovely au revoir. We *would* meet again.

"Danica, bring your boy to my office in an hour. You and I have a lot to talk about."

She nodded and led her boy upstairs to her suite. On her way out of the dining room, I called across the room, "Your slave needs a name."

"So does yours," Danica said and pointed at #99.

It was going to be a delightful day.

Two Months Ago

CHAPTER 16

The Begging

NOVA LOOKED NERVOUS when she delivered the message that arrived via a contact form on my private website. My girls usually handle emails from the website and only the important ones get my attention. Deciding what is and is not important is Nova's task. She had done a passable job for the past few months so I read the printout after she crept through the slave and squatted at my feet.

The inquiry wasn't just important. But it was surprising.

The message claimed to be from a tech executive I'd heard of but hadn't met personally. I was suspicious and had the research team My Cop suggested investigate, Their report said they were 98% sure it was from the tech exec's personal account. I was reading a legitimate email from a well-known, recently-wealthy Silicon Valley type.

He wanted an audience. An hour, he wrote. He said *please* and *I bet you get lots of requests* several times. I was interested. A remote slave like him was worth an hour for a video call.

I had Nova set it up and as usual, I could see him and he could only see the big *A* icon. I recognized him and he showed me his office, replete with the company logo and letterhead on his desk. After the short tour, I asked him what he wanted.

"Ma'am, I am grateful you agreed to talk to me. I'm sure you get many requests for your time. Thank you for granting some of your valuable time to me."

OK, this was starting out well. He was polite, appreciative and called me Ma'am. When I deal with new potential slaves, I let them talk. They are always nervous and I get a lot of useful information when they sputter. This one wasn't sputtering.

"I am owned by the most wonderful woman. If you thought I wanted to enter your slavery, that's not the case. Any man would be lucky to be owned by you. But I have a different question. A different kind of wish."

Owned? Another Domme's slave wanted to talk to me? Was something wrong with his owner? Was she ill or — oh my god — injured?

"Go ahead," I said.

"I would do anything for her. She has a dream and I have the means to give it to her. But I need help to turn it into reality. I researched who the best person was to help me with this. You know, the top Domme, the one everyone aspires to be. That was unquestionably you."

He was winning me over with obvious flattery.

"I've read every one of your books. I hope you consent to give me some of your best advice."

"Like the Queen told Alice, start at the beginning, tell me your story and when you are done, stop," I said.

He was raring to go. "My owner's dream is to own a large estate filled with male slaves and create her version of Amityworld. That's the dream I want to give her. I have the money. Plenty of it. I bought the land already. Everything else is what I can't do by myself."

Whoever she was, she was one lucky Domme. If his story checked out, I was inclined to mentor the boy. Not on video. In person.

I wanted to settle a mystery first. "What's her name?"

"I don't call her by her name," he said and looked down at his shoes. Of course he didn't use her name. That's not a slave's right. Most of us tell our slaves how to address us.

"I am allowed to call her Ms. Danica."

Aha! I had heard of a fledgling Domme up north with a small stable and big plans. When I first heard her name, I had My Cop see what he could find out about her. His reply was short. "Legit," he said. From what my friends talked about on our video chats, she was up-and-coming, a woman we all wanted to meet. And check out for ourselves.

"Tell me exactly what you are asking me to do." When giving slaves instructions, it is always more productive to use as few words as possible. They are easily confused.

"I have the acreage already. I need to know what to put on it. What kind of buildings? What goes in them? My architects have the main house designed. It's beautiful, big and beautiful. But the building her slaves will sleep in? A place for her to train them? That's where I need your help. Your expertise. Everyone talks about your estate like it's heaven."

It *is* heaven. It's Amityworld.

"I will be pleased to assist you in the planning. However, not on video."

"I accept any conditions you demand. I am indebted to you for your gracious offer." His words sounded genuine. He face confirmed it.

My Cop's report noted he had his own plane. This was a good opportunity for him to use it.

"My personal girl will set a date for you to arrive at a private airport and she will send a limo to bring you here. Plan to stay four weeks. You will understand Danica's needs only after you spend time in my world."

His face lit up. "I am SO grateful. Thank you, thank you! My time is yours."

Yes, his time would be mine. So would the rest of him.

"Does your owner have a name for her new realm?" I asked.

"Destiny," he said.

My next question would change his life.

"Hers? Or yours?"

CHAPTER 16

Danica's Boy

DANICA'S BOY ARRIVED and I treated him like any new slave. He was scrunched up in the way back of the limo and told to strip. Several contortions later, he was clad in a thin gray jumpsuit with a single snap holding it closed. Mostly closed. He wouldn't wear it very long.

Once he was uncrated in the transport garage, I sent Nova to run him to the Intake building. She needed the exercise and besides, I enjoy watching her huge breasts and fat layers bounce. Danica's boy followed her until they reached the door. She left him there. I wanted to see how he handled being admitted and undergoing the customary medical checkup all new slaves are given. He was scheduled to be here for a month, so removing his body hair was essential.

The first time new slaves meet me in person is when I shave their heads. For many males, it's their first taste of ultimate submission. To me. There is something about removing their head hair that challenges most men. Especially when the razor is in my left hand.

A voice on the speaker said, "Enter," and the boy turned the door handle. He was about to walk into his new reality and for all his fame and wealth, he was clearly nervous. That's how a new slave should feel. Uneasiness keeps them on their toes.

The voice on the speaker told him to sit and the only furniture in the room was an exam table. Once he complied, Emma walked in with her pink stethoscope hanging around her neck. Emma has examined several new slaves so she launched into her regular routine. She does it silently. New boys have to learn to obey a single pointing finger.

Emma unsnapped the jumpsuit and it fell on the exam table. The boy was naked and would stay that way for the month he was here.

She took his blood pressure and heart rate, measured his soft cock and read the length out loud. She always deducts an inch. Males are sensitive about their length and their faces reveal their fragile egos. His was no exception.

Emma twirled her finger and the boy flipped onto his belly. She reached under his crotch and pulled him up on his knees. Two taps to his ankles spread his legs apart. I had a clear view on my monitor of his raised ass.

One of my medical girls made sure he was lubricated. That's not a part I need to watch. I switched monitors so I could see his face when she used extra time with all of her fingers inside him. I've seen that face dozens of time. He gritted his teeth and closed his eyes. But he endured it without complaint.

After Emma inserted the camera and I had a good look inside to make sure there was no anal damage, she took pictures of him inside and out for his file. Once she gave him a clean bill of health, he was sent to esthetics for hair removal. My girls waxed him from his neck to his toes. He made his first sounds during that process. A few groans punctuated by loud grunts. At least he didn't scream.

Nova sent a note that the golf cart was ready to take me to Intake to finish his removing his hair. I leashed her to the back of the cart for exercise. Once in a while, I looked behind me to see her massive legs churn and her weighty bosom bounce.

When I was settled, a girl pulled the boy by his cock and put him on his knees at my feet. His skin was red from the waxing and his ass was still tender from the camera and rectal exam. Ordinarily, I don't speak to new slaves until their heads are shaved. I had a few words for this one.

"Memorize everything you just experienced."

He nodded. That was another task on his to-learn list. My slaves nod with their asses, not their heads.

I had him lay on his back on the table. One of my girls locked him into place and handed me the electric razor. She tilted the table so his head pointed down. I turned the razor on and grabbed a handful of his light brown wavy hair. I pressed the edge of the razor to the top of his forehead. A lightbulb went off over his head.

That was only the second time he said anything since he landed. It sounded something like "ohgodohgod." When the front was gone, I flipped the table over so he was looking at the floor. It was covered with tufts of his hair. I shaved the back and sides. I looked at the pile of hair and saw that some of it was wet with his tears. Males have a thing about head hair.

I have a thing about absolute submission.

Besides, keeping slaves bald equalizes them. There are no egos in my stable.

I was done with him for now, so I gave him back to Emma to inject soft plastic and form his first ass plug. It's important to know a slave's capacity before attaching him to a stretching machine. You don't want slaves with damaged asses. They are unrentable and useless.

A few hours later, Nova crawled in to give me her late-morning report. The last item was the new boy's status. He finished initial Intake and had been through two obedience lessons. I won't see a boy in my office who hasn't learned the fundamental rules.

"Put him outside the slave door," I said.

A few minutes later, a panting Nova set the boy on his hands and knees in the hallway facing the closed slave door. I replied to two email requests for my time before I opened the half-door.

He fit through it easily. A month of calisthenics would fix that.

The boy crept to my feet and assumed the proper slave position, the one he learned in his first obedience lesson. On his knees, hands on the floor as far as he could reach and his forehead on the carpet.

He also learned not to speak unless asked a question that required more than a yes or no answer. The second lesson taught him how to nod. With his ass.

After a few minutes of what I predicted was serious contemplation about what the hell just happened to him, I offered my first piece of advice.

"Remember every step you took this morning."

His ass bobbed up and down.

"Extrapolate that backward, from the airport to the slave door to my office. Now you know what Destiny needs to bring in new slaves."

More ass bobbing. He'd never forget every step and what was done to him at each stop on his journey.

"You have been in my world for four hours. It feels like a lifetime, doesn't it?"

This time, his backside moved up and down almost fanatically. He would remember those four hours for the rest of his life. There were 716 left in the month I was keeping him.

"My new slaves spend two weeks in Intake. Yours will be a rapid version, given your situation. If you perform satisfactorily, I might assign you to the slave dorm. For now, you will be isolated at night until I am confident you won't disrupt my stable. You will follow a typical slave schedule."

His ass communicated that he understood and accepted my rules. Really, he had no choice. He might be a good slave now. When I was done with him, he would be an excellent one.

I had one more item to share.

"You will be given one hour each day to meet with my architect and construction manager, one of my remote slaves. He will advise you about buildings and layout. Use that time well."

The boy was trembling. He had a lot to be frightened of and his journey had just started.

-=o=-

After Nova put the boy in his temporary cage next to the Intake building, I kept an eye on him on my monitor. What I saw was illuminating. He was happy being alone in the cage. I made sure he could read his architect's plans even though they were fairly bare. He studied them and made notes for a while, then curled up in a ball and slept. He needed the rest, as much for his body as for his mind.

He talked to himself. Not out loud, but his lips moved and he nodded when he agreed with whatever he said. By tomorrow, his video feed would be sent to an interpreter to decipher.

When I first met him on video, he told me how his owner wakes him in the morning. With a whip. He was proud to show me the remnants of the stripes she drew on him. What I saw was a talented hand at work. And a potential problem.

When Danica bought new slaves, she would not have time to devote to him every morning. He had to come to grips with the fact that he was no longer her only slave. That he was one among many and had no right to expect much of her attention. He might as well learn that here and now. Danica would have enough on her plate. She didn't need a sad boy who felt neglected.

The easiest way to strip a slave of worrying about something he had no control over was to take away something important from him.

That afternoon, I erased his concept of time.

CHAPTER 17

THE FIRST DAY

THE SMALL CAGE in the windowless room that confined him was absolutely dark. When he opened his eyes, he had no idea how long he slept or if it was day or night. The measurement of time he used to use, when his owner whipped him, told him it was morning. For the month he was spending in my world, he didn't need to know that. He had to focus on where he was at that moment and to get busy with what he was told to do.

New boys learn the schedule in the two-week Intake process. They adjust to changes in their schedule so they don't get lazy. They sleep when told, are woken up and perform the tasks assigned to them. Sleep and wakeup times change every day. That's why there are no windows in the Intake building or the stable dorm.

My girls alerted me when he opened his eyes. He'd been asleep for two hours and it was late in the afternoon. My stable was completing their assigned work, putting tools away, closing software, finishing kitchen duties and cleaning every room in the main house. Physical fitness was next for them, followed by their third meal and ending with their last assigned piss-and-shit time. That closed their usual day.

Today's schedule ended with the milking machine. The stable never knew when it was their time but they all looked forward to having their cock cages unlocked for the few minutes it took to drain them. Some of the newer ones still hoped they would be allowed an erection but the longer-term ones knew better.

There are no unordered erections in my world.

Danica's boy would undergo all of it but on the timetable I set for him. Every time was roused awake, he followed a strict schedule.

Wakeup inspection was first, then morning calisthenics and the first piss-and-shit time. No one slave, not even a temporary, is excused from his daily tasks. I had Jack post the schedule on his cage door. There were no times listed, just duties.

He was still groggy when Jack rattled the cage bars with a short carbonite whip. She was dressed in her work outfit, a vest that stopped below her breasts and a leather thong with a slit where it split her lips. When she's working, she wears her ever-present leather boots.

"On your feet!" she said.

The boy was disoriented. It took too long for him to stand up. Jack swung the cage door open and marched in. Two swats on his balls got him on his feet fast.

Jack put him through an abbreviated morning exercise session. He puffed his way through it. My boys count their reps out loud. It reinforces their similarity to each other. There are no prima donnas in the slave dorm.

When the session was complete, he looked at Jack and pointed to his genitals. She pretended not to understand his motions even though what he wanted was clear. The boy had to pee and there was no toilet in his cage. But there was a bucket.

On his third try to tell Jack his urgency, she pointed to the metal pail, looked at him, then at the bucket. With a sigh, he picked it up and Jack swatted his ass with the whip. She pointed to the floor. He set the bucket down and attempted to aim into it. Another swat, another pointing finger. The boy knelt and hung his cock over the edge.

Like I said, every boy I own learns my rules.

The rest of the day and well into the night put him through a typical schedule. He cleaned the stable's bathroom, emptied toilets and scrubbed them spotless. He was fed greens from the garden and a soy-based protein shake. Following that was an hour with my architect before he was sent to run across the fields to the training building.

I had two goals for his visit to the remodeled building. First, he needed to see it before he could design one for his owner. More than that, he had to feel it. There's only so much a boy can learn through sight. My training building was planned carefully to handle a dozen slaves at a time. Or just one.

I made sure he met three of its features.

While he hung from the crossbeam, I encouraged him to think about the counterweights and backups for the wrist cuffs. Even though I permitted him to speak, he had trouble getting words out after each stroke of my fiberglass cane. He felt how close-fitting the wall cages are and it was up to him to figure out why I had them made only 12-ish inches deep with round cutouts in the front and back. A small whip on his cock and balls that I pulled through the front hole told him not only what that cutout was for but also let him feel what I could do with the one in the back. He realized its function when I pulled the cage from the wall and rotated it.

The new punishment benches were his final experience of his first session. He certainly felt how firm the bench was after he was strapped on it and my single-tail kissed his asscheeks. But it was the last phase that told him what words could never express.

That's when I knew for sure what his second skill was. It's something male slaves try to hide, even from themselves.

The boy was an ass slave.

I had a girl inject him with a lube kit and ordinarily, the injection is a mere prelude to the daily ass expanding new slaves undergo. Slaves rarely react to the long tube that reaches well inside them. A few gasp, some are embarrassed. Very few get excited.

This one did. When the girl worked the injector deep inside, he made a noise I recognized as the first notes of his slave song. Not a grunt, not quite a groan. The boy moaned. That told me what he was.

With daily time on the expander, he would be able to take a large penis without my being concerned with an anal injury. More than that, he had the makings of a highly rentable product. All he needed was a more flexible ass. New boys spend time on the mechanical expander. They are locked to the bench and lubed, then the machine's tip is aligned with its target. The speed is adjustable as is the size of the tip. Its only drawback was that it kept boys from working while it ran its program.

That's why my developers created the new transportable expanders that can be worn when a boy is working. After he had a more pliable ass, I'd have him fitted for one.

When the hour was up, I flipped the bench over and took a close look at his organs. It's a benchmark I use to evaluate a new boy's Intake success. I buy sexual slaves, the ones whose cocks react to me. They're much easier to train than erection failures. It takes one small item to propel them into submission.

My cock cages. The new ones with telescoping sounds.

A boy earns his cage after Intake. This boy was ready for his. I love the sound when the lock snaps shut.

CHAPTER 18

Enduring Emma

LEGS APART, ANKLES LOCKED and spread-eagle on the bench, Danica's boy was terrified. It's the state I keep my slaves in. Fear. Trepidation. A bit of terror. When they are alone with me and restrained, they are living their dream — and their nightmare.

"Aussie, heel!"

My pet dog followed me out. That left the slave on the bench absolutely alone.

I had a girl turn down the lights and left the boy alone for five minutes. Being by themselves and unable to move an inch churns a new slave's emotions. Did I abandon him? Was I going to sell him? Punish him? Worrying about what will happen to them next keep boys in line. It's also why a boy has to earn his cot in the dorm with the rest of the stable. Isolation wreaks havoc on their minds. It also makes them very compliant.

When I returned, the boy was trembling. It was only a few minutes before his second piss-and-shit time, so I wasn't surprised that he wet himself. Of course he was mortified, exactly as I planned. If I left him alone much longer, he would be blubbering tears. They all do.

It was late but still his first day, so rather than have a short-term nearly hysterical boy, I patted his bald head. Knowing I was there calmed his frenzy. The tears stopped, the frantic breathing slowed. I grabbed his cock in my fist.

It was hard. He was enjoying the last erection he would have for the rest of his time in my world. If Danica was smart, and I believed she was, it would be his last one for a long time. A very long time.

It was time to put him in a training cock cage. The forever one would follow when I assigned him to the slave dorm.

I yanked his shaft through the ring and squashed his testicles to fit through. The ring sat flat against his hairless groin. The hard cock had to be compressed to get it into its new tiny home. I held his organs in my hand and told him what his future held.

"Slaves do not have erections unless I order one," I said. "This is your last one. I hope you enjoyed it."

I snapped the cage shut. There were only two ways to open the lock. One was the control box in my office. The other was in my hand.

He was powerless before I caged him. He was absolutely helpless when I locked the cage. From peeing to feeling any touch on his cock, he was totally dependent. On me.

Taking ownership of a male is a remarkable feeling. It was late and I suddenly felt hungry. The chefs sent two small desserts to my suite as their final exam but I had a taste for something else.

I jolted Nova. With her breasts and belly joggling, she puffed her way into the training building.

"Fetch Zayn and My Cop to my rooms."

Aussie barked. Whenever My Cop is with me, Aussie is relegated to being my secondary protector. Aussie knows that when My Cop is in my suite, he is busy pleasing me and the dog takes over. His arf told me he was prepared to take charge.

The boy on the bench quaked so hard, I was doubly glad the new benches' restraints were upgraded.

I left the training building and rode to the main house. Aussie ran behind the cart, one of the few times he is allowed to be on two feet. Exercise is good for dogs, especially before bed. Nova plodded behind him, huffing and puffing the whole way.

-=o=-

Jack unlocked the caged boy and sent him to his next scheduled task. He worked all night, ate a second meal, did his afternoon fitness workout and had his second piss-and-shit session. Emma reported he had not moved his bowels in almost 20 hours and asked permission to empty his colon.

New slaves usually need cleaning out. As far as I was concerned, the first cleansing this boy was facing is nothing more than a simple semi-medical procedure that I have little interest in. After a slave earns his place in the dorm, it's a twice daily requirement. My attention isn't on the outcome, that's a given. I watch the line of slaves waiting their turn at the small toilets they share. Each boy is timed and if he doesn't perform, he is sent to Emma who has her ways of clearing a boy's colon.

Given the alternative, my boys struggle to shit within the time limit. Daily enemas take care of most of them. The rest? When they are released from Medical, their colons are empty. So is any sense of pride. It must have something to do with the rectal tube's length and the shock it propels into them. The only thing I care about is that it works.

Constipated boys don't work at full capacity.

Jack wrapped a mask over his head and dropped the boy at the Medical door. She jogged away, her leather boots clomping with each step. The boy was worn out after enduring the most physically and mentally demanding 22 hours of his life. The isolated cage in the windowless anteroom probably looked good to him now. That's not how it works in my world. The schedule must be obeyed.

A medical girl let him in and put him on an empty exam table. Two other tables held fully-masked, caged but otherwise naked slaves. One was being seen for oozing stripes on his ass, a result of a few minutes at the business end of my single-tail. Had the boy finished his work on time, he would be in the dorm, finishing his exercises and put to bed. The other one's urine indicated a possible UTI. Checking urine output is one of Emma's jobs. She seems to enjoy holding the cup while she collects the samples.

Emma was seeing the ass-oozer. She had him on his knees, ass up and forehead on the exam table when the new boy walked in. Emma told him to assume the same position as the boy she was tending to. Ass up. Face on the table.

The boy with the suspected infection was on his back, feet attached to stirrups. Two asses to take care of and one penis was Emma's idea of afternoon delight. Aside from having no egos, my slaves also have no privacy. It levels them. None are better or worse than the others. Humiliation is a useful tool to equalize males.

She coated the oozing ass with antibacterial ointment and ordered the boy to stay as he was while it dried and she would take a second look. The second boy's penis had to be drained for the sample Emma needed. That called for a catheter. She threaded it into him and ignored the boy's wails. Once she had enough, Emma left the tube in place and turned to the new boy.

"Failure to shit," the girl told Emma, who broke into a grin.

"We'll fix that right away," Emma said. "Take a bag out of the refrigerator and hang it on the pole."

Keeping enemas cold is one of Emma's rituals. She says it works better and faster when it's below 38-degrees. My only concern is that the boy adheres to his schedule. He failed two piss-and-shit times. That earned him a trip to Emma and her effective treatments. New boys tend to need her ministrations. They have a thing about sitting on a tiny toilet in front of the stable. That problem goes away in time, usually after their second visit to Medical.

Emma lubed the boy's ass with her gloved fingers. Because it was his first time, she noted on his chart, she used an injector as well to make sure he was lubed deep inside. Lubrication flows in Emma's medical unit like a river. She worked the tube all the way into him and released the valve. When the cold contents shot inside, the boy tensed his gut and had his second weepy episode of the day. First days are often punctuated with crying jags. This boy was no different.

While the enema worked, Emma revisited the oozing ass and declared it done. She had him put on tiny panties to make sure the ointment didn't soil his cot or work chair. The pink frills were a nice touch.

Penis boy was emptied, so she pulled out the catheter and clicked his cage shut. He rolled off the exam table, bent almost in half, clutching the cage to comfort his penis. But he felt nothing. Good cock cages prevent any feeling of touch. She had one boy left to deal with.

First-day enemas are more effective when there is an audience. Emma kicked a metal bucket across the room and pulled out the enema hose. She had the boy stand and bounce up and down to make sure the fluid filled every nook and cranny. The new boy eyed the boy in pink-frills and the bent-over male and knew he had to obey. He also learned that Medical — and Emma — are to be avoided at all costs.

That cost is absolute obedience. It's a lesson every slave has to learn and that's why they spend two weeks in Intake.

She pointed to the bucket. He trotted across the room, his fingers in his ass trying desperately not to leak. When he got there, he had only one option. The boy sat on the bucket and shit until he was empty. In front of an audience.

A boy's first day as my owned slave is a never-ending lesson. The ones that learn the fastest are the most contented slaves in my stable.

Danica's Visit

CHAPTER 19

CAGING A SLAVE

DANICA'S SLAVE SPENT two sleep-deprived weeks learning how things work in my stable. He discovered there were many things in his former life that he took for granted. Things that a slave has no use for. Like time. It didn't matter what time of day it was. The only concern a slave has is what he is told to do and when it must be done. The slaves' schedule is inviolate so all of them know what they will do from wakeup until the they are put to bed for the night. What they think is night.

By day fourteen, the boy accepted that he no longer owned his bodily functions, from piss-and-shit to physical fitness. His shoulders and arm muscles were developing and forced runs were building up his legs. He never saw the changes. There are no mirrors for slaves. It helps develop a sense of sameness, what with all of them bald, hairless and muscular.

Danica's boy came to my world with an overgrown ego. Two weeks in, it was gone.

I decided to move him into the slave dorm. He met with the architect and Mason every day and the plans for Destiny were firming up. His first meeting with them after spending two days in the dorm was telling. There would be a slave residence in Destiny that was almost a mirror image of mine. The sections slaves were assigned to made sense after he learned how I group my boys. By skills.

The ass-boys, the ones that are rented to clients who fancy that kink, wear expanders while they sleep. It's an efficient use of downtime. Some clients want one ass-boy for themselves. Others want one for a group. A few want multiples at the same time. That means all of my ass-boys must be ready to go. New boys are attached to a mechanical expander and graduate to the new wearables they can wear all day and night.

He also noted that the mouth boys, the ones with trained lips, tongues and teeth, spend their days wearing mouth masks that measure their sucking ability. The readouts show their sucking intensity and when they achieve a satisfactory level, a bigger plug replaces the small trainer. My tools have more than one purpose. Mouth gags keep them quiet, too.

His biggest takeaway was that my slaves are monitored constantly. Video cameras aren't disguised. Boys know I am watching everything they do. That lesson was driven home when one boy semi-consciously fondled his cock cage in the middle of the night. He wound up on the floor, thrashing and shrieking from the sound's jolts.

Anywhere. Any time. I control my stable.

There were two requirements the boy had to meet before I assigned him to a cot in the dorm. Like every male in the dorm, he needed to be permanently caged. And he had to have a name, one I felt suited him. Danica could replace it when I gave him back to her. Think of it like adopting an orphan puppy. You have to decide if you want the pup to keep the name a former owner gave it or if a new name suits you better.

Caging a new slave in my permanent device is a rite of passage. It tells a boy he passed my initial tests and has entered probation. It also prevents disruption in the dorm. No one can see how big or small a slave's cock is when they are all caged. It makes them feel ungendered, a useful by-product.

I jolted Jack's chip twice. She galloped to the small door to my office, struggling not to rub herself where it hurt. She wriggled in and squatted at my feet.

"The new boy is ready for his cage," I said. That was all I had to say. Jack knew what caging involved and I dismissed her to get everything ready.

The boy hadn't yet visited the punishment building. That's where I lock cages on the new ones and it's the venue I had designed for rare brandings. Branding was the moment my current exclusives became my proprietary boys, the select two allowed in my suite to serve my hunger. They will wear my initial on their sacs forever.

Caging isn't as complicated as sizzling branding irons but merits a small ceremony. Slaves, especially new ones, thrive on rituals. It makes them feel special and fosters equality. A boy ready to wear my cock cage has proved his fidelity and obedience to me. It is a kind of graduation, although I think of it like moving from kindergarten to primary school. Caged boys have a lifetime of education ahead of them for as long as I care to keep them.

When I was driven to the punishment building, Jack had my household girls lined up in a neat row. They were allowed to wear leather thongs with slits in their pussies and vests that revealed their bosoms. Being allowed to wear those outfits was a privilege. Their usual dress fits my three rules: cheap, easy and convenient. They had no use for clothing so collars with their names sufficed. Today was special and they stood tall in their finery.

I walked in front of them, tweaking nipples as they bounced in rhythm. That jiggling is a touch I added when I caged six males the same day. Bouncing breasts is now a caging ceremony staple.

The boy was in position and clearly frightened. Spread-eagle on his back attached to one of the new benches, every piece of him was available to me. Before he was sent here, Jack made it clear he was being run across the grounds to the punishment building, a mysterious place he had heard about but had not yet seen. He had no trouble figuring out what probably happened there.

Three recently-corrected boys were led in to show off the stripes my single-tail drew on them. One at a time, I had them repeat their transgressions out loud for the new boy. They confessed their mistakes in strong voices and told me — and the boy — how they deserved what I did to them in this building. On the benches. Benches exactly like the one the new boy was attached to.

The first recounted what happened. "I failed to complete my work on time," he said. "I must obey the schedule. I am thankful Ms. Amity corrected me with her whip."

He bent over to display his asscheeks. Although I didn't draw blood, the marks were fresh. And painful.

"Sit!" I said.

The boy plopped on his ass and groaned.

"Bounce," I added for good measure.

Lest I use the whip in my left hand on him, he obeyed, grunting each time his ass hit the floor.

Jack prompted the second boy to confess his disobedience with her boot.

"My ass did not stretch enough on the machine to earn one I could wear all day and night. I was not rented for two weeks until I met my goal."

A boy who cannot be rented is worthless. The main reason I bought him was for his pliable ass. Failure to stretch to the next level made him ordinary. I do not rent ordinary asses. They have to be spectacular. My clients are sophisticated and expect top-quality.

"I was grateful for Ms. Amity's correction. My ass was locked to the machine for days. I do not know how many days, just that I was proud when the widest plug fit inside me."

I tapped a button and the wearable expander in his ass widened. He cried out in surprise. I ignored his outburst.

The third boy committed the most serious offense, one that put him on my short list for the next auction or a video sale. His voice carried throughout the building.

"A client rated my performance with only four stars. I should have done better for Ms. Amity," he said.

Rental fees cover the cost of keeping a boy so failure to satisfy a client is a serious offense.

"I deserve the jolts Ms. Amity sends to my cage. They remind me that I must correct my failure."

When a boy is awarded his cock cage, he is made aware of what it can do. The new boy was just informed that my cages are more than chastity devices. A lot more.

Jack ran the three of them back to their work. They were eager to finish their tasks, quickly and accurately. Every slave knows what happens to the ones that require a second trip to the punishment building.

In a word? Expulsion.

When a slave is expelled, he is driven to a bus station a few hours away with a ticket to the city he listed as home on his slave contract. He is dressed in a flimsy gray jumpsuit and given his identification. Nothing else. It's a fate every slave has imprinted on his mind.

The girls were sent back to work, sprinting in a line, breasts and one or two fat layers bouncing. It is a lovely addition to a caging.

That left Danica's boy strapped on the bench by himself.

With me.

Caging a slave is one of the few times I speak to a slave and require him to answer my questions in full sentences. Months later, most recall that conversation fondly and claim it solidified their devotion to slavery and gave them a rock-solid understanding of my ownership. They had a lot to learn about my ownership but lifelong caging is a valuable step in that process.

Jack had removed his temporary cage when she attached him to the bench, leaving him fully naked. The bench kept him from moving even an inch. Judging from his trembling, he was on the edge of panic. That's one of the states I keep my slaves in. They behave when they know what the outcome might be. The three confessors proved it.

I fondled his cock a little to give him a final memory of what touch felt like. Even though he was nervous and scared, like most males in that position, the shaft in my fingers stiffened. I yanked it and the two balls through the electrified ring and pressed the ring against his groin. The permanent cages are small so I squeezed his organs into the little device. All that was left to do was snap it shut.

"Do you pledge yourself — your entire self — to be my slave for as long as I own you?"

It calls for a yes or no answer, but slaves want to say more than that. This is the time I allow them to use full sentences.

"I do. My whole self. Everything I am."

It was heartfelt. It was also typical of what many in his position say.

"Tell me what my ownership means to *you*."

That gave him pause. His quivering slowed and his eyes focused on mine. "I feel lucky that you even want me. I spent my life getting ready to be owned. I don't know where I am or what day it is but I feel safe where I am. With you."

That realization came fairly quickly to this boy. Many slaves do not achieve that level of understanding until after I have their numbers tattooed on their asses. When they serve two full years, a duplicate is inked on their shafts.

My most important question was also my last. "Who are you?"

The boy thought for a while before taking a deep breath and saying clearly and loudly, "I am a slave owned by Ms. Amity."

I snapped the cage shut. The click signified my possession of his body and thoughts. Tears flowed from the corners of his eyes and dripped onto his bald scalp.

"Ms. Amity owns you," I said.

"MS. AMITY OWNS ME," he shouted.

"Yes, I do. For as long as I care to keep you."

CHAPTER 20

THE SLAVE DORM

BEFORE I SENT Danica's newly-caged boy to the slave dorm, he needed a name. A temporary name. Something to put on the daily schedule. A name to tell Aussie which one to fetch or have Nova deliver. I use numbers because they're easier for me to remember, especially when I have them tattooed on their right asscheek. Only the keepers get that number tattooed on their shafts.

Numbers categorize them and what they do. The newest ones are in the 100s until I assign them to a group. Lower numbers reflect their value to me. The lowest numbers are the ones most beneficial to my bottom line. Numbers are a convenient way for my clients to request a particular rental and I can have Jack bring me the 20s, for example, if I want to use the biggest cocks as demos in a Parlor.

Big cocks generate big revenue.

I gave #99, a recent addition, a temporary number. He had the potential to fit into several categories so his ultimate classification would take some time. Besides, he had the makings of a potential personal boy and if he served me well in that capacity, perhaps an exclusive. One day.

While I rode back to the main house form the punishment building, I jolted Nova to tell Jack the boy was being run across the grounds to the stable. I settled on his name.

Danica's boy would be my #55. He was a mix of categories. Slaves in the 50s collection were well-connected in their former lives, some were recurring ass rentals and they were all on my list for targeted skill development. The 50s were set for training to fill the more unusual client requests. Uncommon requests are typical of my male clients.

Those are the ones I insist attend my Parlors before they are permitted to rent my merchandise. They talk to each other. Parlor applications skyrocket when they are treated to a slave with an extraordinary skill.

The fact is that many men, especially the influential and privileged ones, share their darkest secrets with each other. I shine light on them in Parlors and later, in the new cabins. Video keeps my boys safe.

I watched #55 run behind Nova to the stable entrance and tried not to laugh at her bouncing bosom and belly. The newly-named boy had no trouble keeping up. Two weeks of three-times-a-day training was transforming what was an out-of-shape tech mogul into a worthwhile rentable. He was still less developed than most of my stock but now that he was living with them, the slaves I used as trainers would give him extra work. Failure to make progress with #55's build would earn the trainers a trip to the punishment building. That fear made them relentless so every stable boy acquired a physique my clients almost drooled over on their rental applications.

My Domme friends always comment about how solid the boys I sell are. One look tells the buyers there are no discounts on my stock.

#55's entry to the stable followed the same process every new boy undergoes. There is no pecking order. My slaves, no matter their skills or talents, are equal. They follow the schedule, do their work, undergo rigorous calisthenics, are fed and are allowed piss-and-shit breaks. Any disobedience is corrected, usually with an unforgettable trip to the punishment building and a taste of my whip.

When I give them pain, it has a purpose. My purpose is to teach them obedience.

Naked and caged, #55 stood outside the door until Jack let him in. The small foyer is windowless and for new slaves, time stands still. So do they. They kneel in the blackness to let their former lives and current fears wither away until they are empty. Only then can they become what they are now. Nothing. Something to be rebuilt. My way.

I watched him ponder his situation. Males like #55 who are used to being in charge, issuing orders to others and having everything they want, have a lot to give up when they enter my stable. They give up more than things. They cede any feeling of control when they accept mine. That's what #55 was dealing with on his knees in the small dark room.

I've seen many boys before him in the same position. They need time to acknowledge that their former lives are erased. Like I tapped their delete key. When I see a boy concede to that, I press a button that opens the door. Sometimes it takes a while for that ultimate submission to fill the emptiness. Some cry, others shake and shudder. A new world is worth trembling about.

#55 placed his hands on the floor in front of him and lowered his forehead between his hands. He was ready. I opened the door.

When his eyes adjusted to the bright lights, he nudged his head up and saw the opposite of the darkness that previously enveloped him. Bright white tile reflected the vivid overhead lights. The room facing him was wide and long. It was filled with numbered males under Jack's watchful eye. #55 was torn between crawling through the doorway or waiting for an order.

He chose the latter. It was the right choice.

Jack sent a girl to insert earbuds in #55's ears. She reached under his belly, grabbed his new cage and dragged him to an empty slot. Not one of my stable boys glanced at him. They were fully involved in their second daily exercise session and couldn't afford even a look at what she dragged in. Their routines are brutal and timed. They are petrified of failing to finish. Not even a new boy could distract them.

Once #55 was attached to the telemetry that recorded his vitals, his ears filled with instructions. "Jumping jacks, 15, go!"

He looked at the others kicking, thrusting their legs and running in place. A shock from the sound in his penis yanked him into his new reality. If he screamed from the pain, no one would hear him, much less care. The boy had one choice. #55 jumped and clapped his hands when he spread his feet. His ears admonished him. "Count!"

When his second jump and clap was done, he shouted, "One!" He counted louder and louder until he yelled, "Fifteen!" His ears told him that pushups were next and exactly how many he would do. The voice didn't have to remind him to count. Out loud.

All around him, sweaty males were running through their routines, listening carefully for today's changes. There is no normal routine for any of them and they can never predict what their earbuds are going to tell them to do. Keeping my stable in a state of tension forces them to be alert at all times. Expecting the unexpected is their way of life.

When the entire stable was running in place, they were near the end of their second daily physical workout. I have the trainers make the final drill the same for all of them. It's a convenient way for me to know it's the last one before the slaves are sent to their next task. In this case, it was their second feeding.

My chefs prepare nutritious menus for the stable. Healthy slaves work harder, need almost no downtime to rest and finish their work on time. For most of them, getting used to eating well is a big change from their previous diets. The outdoor crews tend the garden and since I started growing vegetables on the estate, my food costs have gone down. So have the number of medical problems. A win-win result.

Boys are fed together. It is one of the few times they are all in the same room carrying out the same task. Because my boys have no contact with the outside world, they don't recognize each other so they don't need to be masked. My exclusives never mingle with the ordinary slaves, so hiding their faces isn't an issue.

Slaves are permitted to chat with each other when they eat. Some prefer not to engage in conversation because finishing their meals is their first priority. They know there is no more food until their next scheduled meal and failure to finish earns them a trip to the punishment building, right after Jack sends a shock into their cocks via the handy sounds in the new cages.

Boys finish their meals. It doesn't matter what they are served.

#55 followed the line of boys from the exercise area to the feeding room. Each boy knew his place and stood on his number taped on the floor. #55 put his feet on his number and looked at the boy to his right. His feet were planted on #99.

They did that nod thing that men do to acknowledge each other's presence. Both were recently caged and in the dorm for the first time. I put them next to each other intentionally. For their first two weeks, neither #55 or #99 lived with the stable. I kept #55 apart to experience slave life so he could design living space for Destiny's new herd of slaves from his own experience.

As for #99, I had plans for him and didn't want him distracted by the other slaves who didn't have his potential.

When it was time for #55 to leave, the few who noticed his absence would assume he was expelled. Like I always say, slaves who assume are always wrong. I wanted to see how #99 handled the concept of here yesterday, gone today. In his former life, #99 led squadrons. Commanders like him make sure no one is left behind. Just like My

Cop made sure #99 was rescued. That's a lifelong code that two weeks of Intake could never erase. It is a quality I look for in an exclusive.

Once I saw how #99 dealt with the temporary slave's upcoming absence, I could decide if the new gel the old man developed was right for him. The new one hollows out a slave, eradicates his 'self,' and leaves a huge hole. Zayn's ancient Asian Master developed the new gel to fix a particular miscreant I rehabilitated but who slipped back into his criminal ways. In his case, it was the bastard who led the group that attacked my friend and put her in the hospital with a year-long recovery ahead of her. With a few Domme friends, we taught them how to behave. I was sure they would never hurt another woman again.

Until one of them did.

The new gel, one I would never sell on my site, had profound effects. I dosed the criminal with it at the closing dinner of the Memphis Auction and handed him over to the woman he injured as her lifelong slave. Unlike the purple or black gels, the new gel was permanent. It carved him out and erased how he knew the world. His new life was a constant challenge to make himself useful to her or his next stop was federal prison.

When #55 left, #99 would be concerned about what happened to him and his current whereabouts. If #99 was a potential exclusive, he was not allowed to be distracted. The decision I had to make — whether or not to dose him with the new gel — was life-altering. His life would be changed forever.

The old man held my hands and warned me that when the gel emptied a man of who and what he was, it was my responsibility to fill him. The criminal was now a devoted slave. He had a role and a purpose.

It all depended on what I wanted #99 to be.

-=o=-

After feeding time, the stable was marched to the milking room, their last stop before being put to bed. The two new boys were last in line. The first half-dozen took their places in the stalls and Jack's girls locked cuffs on their wrists and attached them to overhead rings. No one had to tell them to spread their feet. Except for the last two in line, they had all been machine milked before. Three times a week is their average.

My boys do not ejaculate. Milking takes care of that urge and prevents troublesome behavior. A few of the newer ones still hope that one day they will be allowed to finish on their own. Boys who try to predict their future in my world are always wrong.

Jack alerted me that milking was about to start. She knows I occasionally watch to make sure every boy is emptied. Not that I doubt Jack. There's another reason I flip on one of my monitors. Milking is amusing.

I control the only buttons that can unlock cock cages. One at a time, I pressed each boy's numbered button and the cages opened. The girls spread the sides apart and pushed them down. Six cock cages hung from the rings behind their testicles.

The next step went quickly. Flexible tubes were fit onto their shafts. Once the cocks were covered, milking began.

The machine whirred to life. Tubes contracted and released while the machine's ring moved up and down penises, an inch at a time, until the boys were undulating from the stimulation they missed so much. Hips humped, eyes closed, moans filled the room. A few seconds later, it was done. The tubes sucked the contents and sent it to a basin. Six slaves were empty. One by one, the girls squashed their deflated cocks back into the cages and snapped them shut.

Six more boys were attached and the process repeated until there were only two left. By now, both #55 and #99 knew where to stand and what was going to happen. A boy's first milking is worth recording on video. That's exactly what I did.

Dangling from their wrists, they felt their cages open and the tight tubes stretch over their cocks. When the machine started, they couldn't stop their bodies' reactions. Swaying and humping, they grunted in short-lived pleasure. I told Jack to slow it down a little so I could watch their responses. But in the end, the result was the same.

A few globs were extracted and slurped into the basin. They were done. First-timers often sing their version of a pre-bed lullaby I enjoy. Moans and groans make up the lyrics of the songs slaves sing to me. Tonight's was a duet.

When their cages were locked, they were sent to their cots and the lights in the slave dorm were extinguished. I had a few hours left in my evening and sent for My Cop. I stuffed a few berries in his mouth and let him suck my fingers before I fed him what he was ravenous to eat.

With my single-tail in my left hand, I served him a three-course meal.

CHAPTER 21

Reacquaintance

JUST SHY OF TWO FULL weeks living in the slave dorm, #55 had undergone a substantial transformation. There are signals slaves give off when they fully submit to their new lives and my ownership. It starts with their eyes. They don't look side-to-side when they're on task. They concentrate on finishing their work. Their posture changes. They stand up straight, proud to be who and what they are. Any shyness about their naked bodies vanishes. Their need to be in control disappears. They're calm. And focused.

The most noteworthy change shows up when I send for them one at a time. Being summoned to crawl through the slave door into my office is a mark of honor; after all, their owner sent for them. Whatever I want must be important and they bulge with dignity — not pride — when I pay attention to them. Intimate individual attention.

That's how #55 looked when he wedged his new shoulders through the half door and crawled to my feet. He had no idea why I summoned him. He didn't know what day or even what week it was, so he had no expectations of why I sent for him.

"I agreed to keep you for a month," I said. "That month is up soon. Danica arrives tonight for a visit. She will be here several days."

He kept his forehead on the carpet and waited. Silently.

"You can go home without seeing her and she won't know you were here. Or you can stay. If you stay, I will give you to her and you will no longer be allowed to live with my stable."

When his ass trembled, he wasn't answering 'yes' because I hadn't asked him a question. He was scared. His world was orderly here and he knew how much he was thriving under my control. Two weeks in the stable made uncertainty and ambiguity things of his past. Now they were rearing their ugly heads again.

I don't let my slaves make decisions, other than choosing to be obedient. I wasn't going to let #55 make this one either.

"You don't want to leave," I said. It wasn't a question. "But you want Danica to use you and take you to Destiny to serve her. The only future you want and need is to be her slave."

#55's ass wiggled up and down. In the morning at breakfast, Danica was in for a surprise. This one wouldn't be wrapped in a big bow. It would be on his knees under the table.

-=o=-

Because she had visited Amityworld before, I did not make Danica strip in the limo and go through medical. Nova showed her in the front door and we hugged like old friends. Even Aussie was happy to see her and sniffed her shoes. She patted his head and he arf'ed like the good dog he is. But it was late and she was tired from the long trip in her boy's plane so I had one of the girls show her to her suite and she turned in for the night. We would catch up over breakfast.

I mentioned that I put something special on the menu.

When I rode upstairs to my rooms, I felt satisfied. Content. Her boy's month-long journey into slavery was almost complete. I had #99 fulltime and watched his progress every day. Sometimes twice a day. He definitely had the makings of a personal boy, one who was allowed to attend me privately. Some day he might earn my brand on his testicles. All he had to do was give himself entirely to me, body and mind. I would know the minute he did. Words mean very little. I can feel when a slave crosses into utter submission.

My Cop was working remotely so Aussie was always at my feet. I used Zayn earlier in the day to prepare Mason for his trip to supervise the crews that were building Destiny. My space planners' work was well received by #55's lead architect out west. She was effusive in her praise of the solar and geo-thermal heating systems, a necessity for a place that far north. The underground tunnels were 'brilliant,' she noted. Zayn put Mason in the proper headspace to be away from my world for a few months.

When he was done with Mason, I had Zayn to myself for a few

hours. I slept soundly that night and woke up full of energy.

Before breakfast, I had Aussie fetch #55 and put him under the table near Danica's chair. The dog clenched #55's cock cage in his teeth and ran him across the field. Neither of them broke a sweat. Danica's boy looked much better than when arrived. He sported broad shoulders, muscular legs and arms and the proper slave mindset.

I sent Aussie back to the stable to fetch #99. If a slave is going to learn to be my personal boy, I won't keep him in the stable very long. His training will be strenuous and it takes a boy time to meet and surpass my demands. Not every boy is capable of that much grueling work. Not every boy is worth my time. Very few have the spark that drives them to erase their 'self' and become mine without a drop of indecision. If #99 was going to be elevated to an attic cell, he had to prove it to me. And to himself.

His journey started under the breakfast table at my feet.

Nova escorted Danica down the main staircase and delivered her to the small dining room for our intimate breakfast. I was already there, sipping coffee and finalizing the lunch and dinner menus with both chefs. They seemed to be dealing well with their roles in the kitchen so I left them as equals. As long as their meals were tasty, I had no reason to sell either of them.

Danica and I hugged again and she held her latte with both hands while we chatted about her flight, her plans for Destiny and her boy who was, to the best of her knowledge, away on business. She was right on one count. He was away. Business? He *was* working, just not in the way she assumed.

As usual, a dish of homegrown berries was placed on the table. I picked two and dropped my hand toward #99's mouth. It was the first time he felt my fingers on his lips, a test to see what he would do. His lips parted and I pressed my fingers inside. This was his initial lesson that I will put more than food in his mouth. Sucking must come naturally to male slaves.

I knew he was a good sucker but if he couldn't make my fingers feel special, I doubted his future as my personal boy. How would he do?

He responded in seconds. He sucked. My fingers felt respected. My toes felt warm.

"Danica, feed the slave at your feet."

She looked at me quizzically and probably figured I was loaning her a boy during her stay, so she picked two raspberries from the bowl and dropped her hand. She never looked under the table. I watched her face. Actually, her eyes. First, they were blank. Then her entire visage changed.

Danica was physically in my smaller dining room but emotionally somewhere else. Somewhere enchanting. I could see it all over her face.

That's the thing about real exclusives. You don't have to see them. You *sense* them. You *feel* a genuine exclusive's presence. All it takes it an authentic Domme and a faithful exclusive.

That's what I saw across the table.

"Oh, Ms. Amity, is this my boy?" Danica asked.

I smiled. Her fingers were obviously feeling the face, chest and shoulders of the slave under the table.

"He feels … bigger. Stronger." Her fingers explored more and she said, "Bald! He's bald!"

I refer to it as 'smooth,' but this was her first time touching his bare head so she was entitled to use any word she wanted to describe it. She didn't bother to look under the table. Her hand served as her eyes.

"I LOVE it!" she said.

That slave on his knees under the table better be grateful his owner liked what she felt. The physical fitness he needed so badly was one facet of turning him into a better slave. One his owner was proud and pleased to own. I tapped my fitness trainer's number into my controller and gave him ten seconds of pleasure in his cage. The video I watched later was comical. He stopped in mid-count and drooled. When it ended, he restarted the entire stable at one. Not one of them dared complain.

"The plans for Destiny are with the architect. My construction slave is ready to oversee the crews that will build it. I'm looking forward to an invitation to see the finished product and the slaves you buy."

Danica nodded. "You will be my first guest. Please visit as often as you wish. I'm so grateful for your help."

We chatted for an hour over breakfast and several cups of coffee. I had Nova clear most of my schedule for the next few days so I could show Danica how to incorporate her slave into her new environment. Into her Destiny. I had a video call on tap for her to review some of

Nashville Ned's stock and one or two of Big Mike's merchandise. At this point in her journey, Danica needed meat — slaves — to build up her stable. She also needed a few females to take care of the big main house and attend to her personal needs. Or a eunuch.

That was the second reason I wanted her to extend her stay here. Bringing in one new slave requires a trusted process. Buying a whole crew at once is more of a challenge. My plan was for her buy a few online, have them shipped here and I would show her how to break them so when they were delivered to Destiny, they were ready to work. I was fairly sure she would be amenable to my proposal. If she balked, then she was on her own. But I know my Dommes and I wasn't worried.

Turned out I was right.

The first time she looked at her boy, my temporary #55, she was amazed at his body and kept rubbing his smooth scalp.

"All slaves must be physically fit. You need to buy a trainer. This one — I pointed to one of my girls — is yours for your stay. She can see to all your personal needs. Facials, massages? She's trained. She's yours, use her."

"This is wonderful, beyond that. Spectacular! I can't thank you enough."

She would. One day. When the time was right.

"The girl will drive you to the training building in 30 minutes. We can go over simple slave fitness programs and then look at some equipment you may want to stock up on. My developers on the west coast are expecting your order."

Danica shook her head, trying to comprehend the opportunity I was giving her. It was hard for her to take in all of it.

Danica was going to make an excellent new member of our network. Her boy's devotion and wealth would benefit her and trickle down to other women in our group.

It was a win-win, my favorite kind of game to play.

CHAPTER 22

Equipping Destiny

TRAINING SLAVES, ESPECIALLY new ones, takes many forms. I don't use a single method. A lot depends on the slave's history, his former owners' rules but most of all, the slave himself. That's why most of us are so careful choosing the ones we buy. No one wants a difficult-to-train slave unless he brings a skill our stable really needs. That kind of male often requires an individualized program after Intake.

No new slave is excused from Intake. They go through a full medical exam, body hair removal and anal insert sizing while learning my rules for stable behavior and my expectations. It's a grueling two weeks.

On the occasions I buy females, the process is similar. Like I said, no slave escapes Intake.

Danica was scheduled to visit with Nashville Ned and Big Mike this afternoon on video to see what they had for sale that might meet her needs. Before she looked at their stock, I wanted her to understand how to bring several new boys into her Destiny. Doing them one at a time is hard enough. A truckload required a plan. Besides that, Danica had to be know which of the boys she bought needed special attention.

The timing was uncannily perfect. I had three boys, one of them an applicant, that were scheduled to be delivered tomorrow. One was the boy I won when I took Mike's bet in Memphis, that my gels could break a boy in less than five minutes. The other had a rentable skill I was short on. Red Rick's truck was due in the morning. That meant I could work with Danica on the new slave process today and put it into action tomorrow.

I might even let her shave one of their heads.

We were driven across the field to the training building with #55 and #99 attached to the cart, running behind us. Aussie ran on the side. It's one of the few times Aussie is allowed to be on only two paws. His regular run is on all fours behind the slave entrance to the main house. A vertical run is good for him from time to time. Danica was amazed that her tech executive kept up without huffing and puffing. I chatted with her about the importance of physical fitness for the stable. I reminded her that all my boys do group exercise three times a day.

"Keep your eye out for a trainer. You might want to buy one so the rest of your purchases can be buffed up in a few weeks. When they're fit, they can do more work. Make fitness a recurring item on their schedule. Besides, They'll be much more interesting to look at."

We both laughed. Danica turned to look at the running boys' bodies and said, "That's for sure! I'll remember that. Don't buy eye candy. Make your own."

Exactly. Just like eunuchs.

When we arrived, I gave her a tour before I sent for the demo boys.

"There are reasons behind each section of this building, the way tools are grouped, how the ceiling is reinforced and which furniture I bought. Sometimes I use one boy and other times, multiples. Working with groups saves time. With the number of new slaves you are going to buy, you want to be able to work with several at once."

Danica looked up at the suspension beams. I watched her count how many boys would fit. "A dozen?" she asked.

"From their wrists or ankles, an even dozen. In fact, the beams hold ten if I cage them." I could see her question before she asked it.

"I had cages built for suspension. A caged boy can't hurt himself and it's a handy way to store them until I have time to train them."

'You thought of everything!" Danica gushed.

"Experience," I said. "I've broken and trained slaves for a long time and have dealt with just about every type. The important thing is that you don't simply want to train them. Break them first. Then you can train them."

"Break and train," she repeated. "I understand how important their daily schedule is but that's part of training. They have to be broken before training even starts. That's so sensible it's hard to believe I didn't think of it before."

DESTINY

"You'll have a chance to break some tomorrow," I said. "I'm expecting a delivery. Which tools would you use to break new ones? Where would you start?"

Danica looked at every wall and the ceiling. She walked the perimeter of the room, refreshing her memory of what tools were on the racks from her earlier visit. Then she inspected the benches in the center and finally, the wall that held my gel display in a locked glass cabinet.

"I heard about your demonstration in Memphis. I mean every tool here, every piece of furniture could be used to break new boys. But if a drop or two of one of these gels could do it in minutes, I think I'd start with that."

I knew she had the makings of a great Domme.

"There's no reason to waste time breaking new boys. Would you like to see how some of my gels work with him?"

Danica looked at her boy, the one I called #55, and then at #99. I could see her mind at work.

"I'd love to see what your gels can do. Perhaps you could demonstrate different colors. After all, there are two right here."

I liked the way her mind worked. "Why only two when more is better?"

I jolted Jack's chip and she jogged in with three of my newer boys in tow.

"How about five?" I said and smiled.

Her arms were dotted with goosebumps. She was going to be an excellent Domme one day.

I unlocked the gel case with my hand on the pad. Jack grabbed #55's and #99's cock cages and bent them over a long horizontal bar. The gel I planned to use first would put on a better show when seen from behind. Their faces didn't matter.

"Always lock them down," I said. "Injured slaves are useless. That's another reason to get them fit and pliable. Bend them in half and lock their wrists to their ankles. It's quick and keeps them from falling off the bar."

Her technique was well-practiced. She had all five restrained in minutes.

"Some gels can be injected. A few should be dripped in. Let's start with injectables."

I handed her an injector and a bottle of blue gel, one of the first ones the old man developed. Even though it has a fairly mild reaction, it can be helpful breaking new boys. It teaches them that I control basic things, like their arms and legs. After I put a single drop into each injector, I gave her a piece of advice.

"Times like this are why you want a few females. They're useful for doing unpleasant tasks like lubricating asses. And it saves time." I pointed to two females who were doing just that, one ass after another. They were lubricated in minutes and my hands were clean."

Danica nodded. She understood. I asked Mike and Ned to show her a couple of females if they had any in stock. I doubted Mike had girls. The Old Leather Masters rarely deal in females. But Ned always had a surprise or two up his leather sleeve.

"I'll do this one's ass. He's my #99. You watch and then do yours."

She stood next to me, focused on the asscheeks hanging on the bar.

"Do you use a spreader?" she asked.

"That's one of the best parts of my injectors. I used to spread them but now I don't have to. One less piece of equipment to sanitize. Watch how easily this goes in."

I pressed the tip of the long tube between #99's cheeks and threaded it into him. "You will feel resistance if you miss. Practice until you can slip it in through the anus and touch the rectum. The gels work more quickly that way."

"Then use the red button?"

"That's the one that delivers the gel. Press once for a single dose. Twice for two. This ass is #99, one of my special boys. When one like him breaks, he knows who broke him. That's who he devotes himself to. The others, the ordinary ones, they don't matter. For them, broken is broken."

"Special boys ... special slaves ..." Danica mumbled. "I know what a special slave is."

Yes, she did. His ass was the next one on the bar.

When #99 felt the blue gel's effects, I didn't have to see his face to know he was terrified. A former POW, he knew what being helpless felt like, to be restrained and at someone's mercy. Or lack of it. This was his first experience feeling that way with me. A slave has to trust his owner. Period. A drop of this simple blue gel would tell me — and him — how deep his trust ran. If he was meant to be my personal boy, let alone an exclusive, that trust had to be 100%. Or more. He had to believe I would keep him safe when he was mine.

The blue gel stiffened every muscle in his arms and legs. Oh, he could breathe but he wasn't going to walk anywhere. Or touch anything. Or talk. Or scream. The old man told me it was designed to immobilize but not harm. He explained that when a male gives himself to a woman, specifically a woman like me, he must rely on her, have faith she might beat him, but she would always protect him. A drop of the gel reinforces that even when he is powerless and totally dependent, he is safe in her hands. Or at the end of her whip.

The old man meant my whip. And my hands.

I patted #99's asscheek, the one that would eventually be tattooed with his number. I was surprised that he whimpered. It must have taken everything he had to make that sound.

His whimper told me he knew he was safe and trusted me. His one-note song confirmed it.

"Your turn," I said to Danica.

She pressed the tip between #55's cheeks. It took two tries before she found the opening and threaded the injector into him. Her boy was gasping for air and grunted with each inch he pushed it into him. When it was fully inside, she pressed the button and stared at his asscheeks.

It didn't take long.

One full body spasm later, her boy hung limply on the bar. I put her hand on his ass and she patted it to reassure him she was there. There were two motionless boys with their ankles and wrists locked together when I heard the sound. A soft moan.

I was done with him and gave him back to her. She owned him now.

We used a drop of green to clear the effects. Danica followed me around the long bar so we could see their faces. Both slaves struggled to raise their heads to look at us, their owners. I wiped tears form #99's eyes with my fingers and pressed them into his mouth.

He sucked like there was no tomorrow. His moaning was the chorus of the song he sang to me. When Danica's fingers were in her boy's mouth, they sang a duet to us.

"Trust. You don't want to own a slave that doesn't trust you. He will be dependent on you for as long as you own him. He is in your custody, more severe than a maximum security prison. That's why we break slaves before bothering to train them."

"I get it, Ms. Amity. I understand. Damn, I can *feel* his trust."

Danica was a good Domme already. She would be a much better one after we went shopping this afternoon.

CHAPTER 23

Video Shopping

SHOPPING FOR SLAVES on video is an stress-free way to buy, especially when I'm looking at Mike's and Ned's merchandise. They are both excellent vendors with stellar reputations. Ned always says, "I only deal in first-quality stock." Most of what Mike has to sell are gay or bi-sexual. Ned deals mainly in CIS-gender boys but may have a female or two at times. I don't fuss about a slave's gender preference. They service whoever and however I tell them to. At first I was surprised how well the CIS-gender boys satisfied my male clients, most of whom checked the boy-on-boy box on their rental applications. It wasn't hard to figure out why they'd disclose that kink to me.

All males have a secret craving to live out their fantasies with other males. They just can't admit it to themselves, much less say it aloud. But they divulge it to me because I make their dreams come true. Watching the videos of them spending an hour or more with one or two of my rentals verifies it.

The most elite, privileged and influential businessmen, elected officials all the way to doctors, lawyers and notably judges, are kinky. They have lived in denial so long, when I give them a secure private space and a superbly-trained male of the sort they've fantasized about, they are in heaven. To a male, they come back for more.

Danica needed to fill her stable with multi-talented stock. Money was no object, what with #55 writing the check. Or transferring the funds between untraceable accounts. The afternoon promised to be delightful, at least for Danica and me.

I had the chefs deliver finger food to the theater in the main house.

Once in a while I enjoy a movie there, but its primary purpose is to train my females and household staff how to cook, clean and make beds properly. After they watch training videos, they are scored on how well they perform.

Failure means a pre-programmed series of jolts to their chips, a trip to the punishment building, and if they fail again, expulsion if I can't find a willing buyer. Movie night was daunting for my girls.

The wide monitor and surround sound made us feel like we were sitting in Big Mike's display room. Danica and I could see his lineup of boys, all tagged with their main skills hanging around their necks. Mike held his ever-present tablet so he could read their summaries to us. After a few pleasantries, I introduced Danica and told Mike she was a friend of mine.

He raised one eyebrow. "That's not something you say very often," he said and grinned for the camera.

"Let's get started. Ms. Amity told me you were shopping to fill your stable and had plenty of room. I followed her skillset list to show you only boys with more than one talent, so you get the most for your money."

Danica smiled at Mike and didn't say a word, just like I taught her. Let the seller do the talking. You'll find out more when you're quiet because sellers like to talk.

"The first one is a good size with lots of muscles. He was raised on a farm and knows what hard work is. Cock is decent, about 7 inches and he stands 6-foot 2-inches."

Fairly ordinary, in my opinion. I waited to hear the boy's talents.

"Put him to work in your garden. Grow your own vegetables. It'll save you boatloads of money."

Danica nodded. Gardening is a good skill to buy. But there had to be more before I'd consider paying real money for him.

"And?" I said.

Mike grinned at the camera. "You think I'd show you a one-off boy? Heck, no. You were clear about that. He's a nurse. Well, more than a nurse. He's a P.A. No, not that kind of P.A."

Pierced boys are harder to sell. I'd never buy one.

"He's a — whaddya call it? A physician's assistant."

That was interesting. Real doctors are hard to find and a P.A. could be helpful in a neophyte stable. I muted the audio and spoke to Danica.

"A medical slave is a good idea. He can deal with injuries or bleeding whip strokes to keep them from getting infected."

She said, "I remember my first visit here. Your doctor and her exam. You had a purpose for that rectal check, didn't you?"

I nodded. I always have a purpose. In this case, it was part of an abbreviated Intake for the visiting Dommes. "Equalize your slaves. What humiliates them elevates your control."

Danica's eyes got wide when she understood what my purpose was for the rectal exam and how she could incorporate it into her own version of Intake.

"It certainly worked for me," she said with a half-smile.

"Tell him you're interested," I said. "Mike will put him in a holding bay and you can negotiate price when you've seen the rest."

I turned on the audio. Danica expressed her interest and Mike moved to the next boy in line.

This one was a huge piece of meat. Every part of him was enormous. Shoulders, arms, thighs and that cock had to be at least 8-inches soft. But he had to have something besides bulk so we listened to Mike's sales pitch.

"Eye candy, right? You can rent this one for a big fee to your clients who want to be dominated. More than that, the small clients will love turning the tables and make the big ones crawl. There's no bigger smile than a fancy guy jabbing his little shaft into a colossal ass."

I've met many of Mike's brothers at his compound in the mountains. He invited me to one of his get-togethers in exchange for a single-tail demonstration. He even decorated one of the cabins in my favorite color and gave me a passel of slaves to use while I was there. At dinner, I found out he made his brothers shower and clean up for my visit. They're great guys and I still keep in touch with some of them. One is the volunteer whose ass I striped in every direction when I taught them how to throw a whip without drawing blood. Now he and I have a special relationship. An expert whipping will do that, even to an Old Leather guy.

I did a private show afterward for the Old Leather guys who wanted to draw blood.

But this boy on the screen? Rentability is one thing. What other talent did his giant have?

Danica said, "Yes, of course, big ones sell. What else can he do?"

"Sounds like you've been hanging around Ms. Amity," Mike said. We all laughed because it was true.

"This may surprise you, given the size of his cock and other parts, but he's a lawyer. Well, used to be a lawyer. Actually, he still is. His previous owner kept him up-to-date."

"What field?" Danica asked.

"Glad you asked," Mike replied. "Two specialties. Contracts for one. Get this. The second is online privacy."

If Danica didn't buy him, I was going to.

"Interested," she said very quickly.

Mike had the boy taken to the holding bay and then showed us the rest of his merchandise. In the end, Danica bought four. In addition to the garden boy and the lawyer, she picked up the medical slave and an accountant. It was a good start.

"Got any females?" I asked.

"Pffft," Mike sneered.

I told him to make arrangements with Red Rick to ship them to me tomorrow and then to Destiny in two weeks when the Intake building was finished. He and Danica could share account numbers later in private. Mike was so thrilled with the sales, he didn't complain about the double shipping.

Danica and I snacked on the goodies my chefs delivered before we looked at what Ned had for sale. She wasn't flustered at all, like buying four slaves on video was second nature to her. If buying from Mike was a commonplace thing to do, perhaps I should challenge her Domme skills on the next review.

Very little is run-of-the-mill in my world. I didn't want Danica to become a careless buyer.

"Aussie, fetch the two new cages," I said.

The dog crawled to the slave door and had to contort himself to get his big shoulders through it. He returned in a few minutes with a leather leash clenched in his jaw and crept to my side. The two leashed slaves behind him had to twist and turn to fit through the opening before they got into proper position. #99 was spread out at my feet. #55 did the same for Danica.

"Ms. Amity, I love what you've done with my boy! I never would have imagined he could be this well-built. I'm going to make it a requirement for my new stable."

Of course she would.

"You'll get higher prices when you sell them," I said.

That's when I noticed #55 was shivering even though it was comfortably warm in the theater. Danica laid her hand on his scalp absentmindedly and felt him shaking.

"Why is he doing that?" Danica asked.

The movement under her hand was exactly what I wanted her to notice. She and I could video shop all afternoon and buy all kinds of merchandise. Her boy was happy to pay for all of it. Intellectually. He heard her say two things that drilled into his core.

The first was "my new stable." The second was "when you sell them."

#55 had to learn he was going to be only one of many slaves Danica owned. They would be kept at Destiny, just like him. She would use and enjoy them. That meant she would have less time for him.

And then there was the idea of being sold. We buy and sell slaves from time to time, just like Danica was going to do with Ned in a few minutes. It was obvious that #55 had never even considered he might be sold.

Teach your slaves that they are not permanent. That kind of tension keeps them on their toes. Slaves are not guaranteed anything. That was what Danica and her boy were about to encounter.

"Are you ready to visit Nashville Ned?" I asked. "Your boy will be fine. Ignore him. We're shopping!"

"Let's spend some money!" Danica said with an evil smile.

The huge monitor flickered to life. Ned filled the screen and I introduced Danica as my new friend. Ned nodded and said, "Pleased to meet ya!"

"We already bought a few today and you're our last call. You better have something special — something distinctive — or this will be a short call."

"Ms. Amity, you know I carry the gol-darn best. First-rate stock. You betcha I've got the finest merchandise in the continental U.S."

Ned is a country boy from Tennessee. You can hear the twang in everything he says.

"Watch what this one can do. Second to none."

Danica leaned forward when one of Ned's boys dragged a body by its shaft in front of the camera. We saw a closeup of a crotch. Ned grabbed a ruler and measured it. "Eight inches. Soft even," he said.

Big cocks are rentable of course but they're fairly common. Surely Ned's slave had more to offer than that.

"What can he do that I might need?" Danica asked. It was well said and very close to what I taught her. Ask questions and make the seller explain.

"Well, Ma'am, you can see how he's built. Used to be a football player. You know, in the pros."

Neither Danica nor I cared one whit about football. There had to be more or Ned wouldn't have bothered making this boy first.

"But I wouldn't show you a one-tricker. Ms. Amity's boys are known 'round the globe as the most built up you can buy. How do they get that way? Well, she has them trained, of course. By a trainer. A slave trainer."

Ned let that sink in. Danica studied the boy's body as the camera panned out to show us every angle. Ned bent him over and had a boy spread his asscheeks for a closer look.

"Interesting," she said. "Let me see him work."

Good for her! Put the seller on the defensive. Make him prove his claims are true.

Ned barked at the boy on the screen. "Gimme ten!"

The boy hit the floor and did ten effortless pushups marine style, the ones where he clapped his hands each time he propelled his upper body off the floor.

"How good a trainer is he? I don't have time to oversee slave exercises. Can he deal with reluctant slaves?"

"Of *course* he can. Very effectively. Watch this. Ain't none of my boys ever think of backtalking this one."

Ned played a short video of the boy leading a stable workout. About 30 seconds in, one of them couldn't get the tenth pushup done and collapsed on the floor. The boy marched over to him, grabbed a fistful of his hair and dragged him up and down. "Ten!" he said.

"I'll take him," Danica said. It took a lot of effort not to smile into the camera.

"What else do you have?" I asked.

Another boy was lugged to the screen by his cock. His fairly small cock. This boy better have premium skills because no one I know would buy something that small. He was short, too.

"I know what y'all are thinking. An itty bitty boy. Sometimes big things come in small packages."

Having bought and sold slaves for years, I knew that was true. What mattered was just how big the boy's talents were.

"He used to be owned by — get this — British royalty. Not in the royal family. More like one of them uppity types that run the government."

The Brit who used to own this boy? I bet his first name was "Lord."

"Are you showing me a butler? Whatever could a slave like that do for me?" Danica's voice edged on testiness.

Out of camera range, Danica snuck a grin in my direction. She knew what she was doing. If she bought him, Ned would have to drop the price because he insulted her. Not on purpose, but a poor choice of words nonetheless.

"Oh HELL no!" Ned roared. "This little boy was the big guy's fantasy. He took care of everything. Everything! From shaving the big guy's balls to cleaning his ass, all the way to bathing and dressing him. Soup to nuts."

His double-entendre wasn't lost on us.

"There are no males I own who need dressing," Danica said. "Is dressing slaves your sales pitch?"

Ned stopped smiling. Danica wasn't getting it. I knew what she was missing.

"Can he do that for an entire stable?" I asked.

"You betcha! I know you keep yours hairless and kinda thought your friend might, too. She needs a slave who's trained to do that. Wait till you see what he can do with a pair of tweezers."

Ned shuddered in mock fright. A lightbulb went off over Danica's head while she rubbed her boy's smooth head and chest with her fingers.

"He's a maybe. Put him in a holding pen till I see the rest."

Danica learned a valuable lesson. You have to see the big picture, the staffing that all parts of a proper estate require. Besides, this boy was probably cheap. Your bottom line will welcome a low-cost slave with a skill you can use. Heck, she might even be able to rent him out to clients who dream about being hairless but don't want to deal with the itching when it's done badly.

My clients must have hairless pubic areas to use my boys. If they don't take care of it before they arrive, my girls take care of it when they are unloaded in the transport garage. After one session having their crotch hair waxed and plucked, they never forget to have it done before they visit.

Ned showed us several more boys and Danica did an admirable job of inspecting them on video. By the end of Ned's display, she had three in the holding pen and we were close to saying goodbye.

"I've got one more. You oughta see him before you go."

Ned is a natural salesman. But he carries first-rate stock and occasionally comes up with something unexpected.

"Let's see it," I said.

A body was dragged by its cock and positioned in front of the camera. We saw its ebony skin, decent arm and leg muscles, a flat belly and when Ned turned him around, a protruding set of asscheeks. Tight asscheeks.

"He's a virgin," Ned said. "Not just that, he'll do anything if you agree to fix him."

Oh, my goodness! We were looking at a potential gelding. Sexless males make handy personal boys and are also frequently requested to rent. It's expensive to create them but they sell for routinely high prices. I know. I've sold several eunuchs I've created. I wondered if Danica realized what prices desexualized males can get at auctions. And what a neutered slave could do for her personally.

Ned read his summary. "Only one owner who trained him in fashion, makeup, hair, the whole nine yards. At home, the boy dressed the owner's females, y'know, models and the like. Took care of everything they wanted. And everything what the owner told him to do. But he didn't want to spring for the cost of sterilizing him. I had you in mind when I bought him, Ms. Amity."

I like sellers who are considerate of my needs. But I had one eunuch and just bought another to spay. I saw how Danica admired my eunuch last time she was here. This was her chance to create one of her own.

"What's his second skill? Danica asked. Good for her. Even though she wanted him — I could feel it — she stuck to the rules I taught her. Never buy a single-trick slave.

"Get this. He's a gymnast. Bends in every which way you can imagine. When he's not taking care of your needs, he's very rentable."

That was for damned sure! My male clients go gaga over bodies that can contort in every direction. A twisted-up former male who used to have a cock and balls would be high on their request lists. All Danica needed was before and after video of the boy bent into the same shape. With and without genitals. Maybe with a tiny vagina.

But Danica was new at buying and also had to perfect her Intake process. I wasn't sure this was the best time to add a potential gelding to her stable. She's a big girl and can make her own decisions, so I sat back and waited to hear her response.

"Thanks for showing me this possibility, Ned. I have a full plate, slaves to take in and a brand new facility to house and use them. It's quite expensive to do all of that. Perhaps I can use him but it depends on the price."

Brilliant. Simply brilliant. Fluttering her eyelashes didn't hurt, either.

"In light of all that, I don't want to over-burden a friend of Ms. Amity. I'll give you my rock-bottom price. Plus a discount for buying more 'n one."

She had Ned in the palm of her hand. I let her negotiate prices and finalize the sales. For that kind of money, Ned didn't mind at all shipping them to me and again in two weeks when Destiny's construction was finished.

We had two hours before dinner. I jolted Nova to deliver Zayn to my suite and pointed at Aussie. He clamped his teeth on #99's cock cage and followed me upstairs.

I was famished. But not for food.

Dinner and Dessert

CHAPTER 24

Feeding My Hungers

THE FIRST TIME I allow a slave into my suite means that he has caught my eye and the next hour tells me if he can meet and exceed my demands. Correction and discipline for the ordinary stable plays out in the punishment building. Then there is the kind of whipping that I do only behind my closed doors. It was time for #99 to have his first adventure with my single-tail. What I had to find out was if he ready for it. Really ready.

That's why I summoned Zayn. With Zayn nearby, my senses are on high alert. Not like red flashing lights on the Enterprise. It's a feeling. I can feel Zayn's warmth. The old man, his Tantric guide, calls it his aura. He had Zayn transfer his aura to me and when he needs it, I feed some of it back to him.

The new leather cock cages I designed for my exclusives and sewn by my Memphis leather guy worked perfectly. He left a space where they are branded so I can see what he called a "very elegant A." I can feel it too. When I trace Zayn's brand, I know if he's balanced or if he needs to be fed a teaspoon of his own energy. He stood in front of me and spread his legs. That's his position when I send for him.

I felt the big *A* under his ball sac and heard his delicious moan. He was perfectly balanced. Zayn was going to need every ounce of his aura during the next two hours.

I pointed at #99 who was facing the wall on his knees in the corner. Zayn understood what I was telling him to do. I rarely need words to communicate with Zayn.

Zayn opened his kit and took out a few bottles of oils and small dishes for the herbs he would use. While he busied himself with the preparations, I put my hands on #99's muscular shoulders and stepped my boots between his ankles. Zayn traced circles on #99's bald head with his oiled fingers and I felt the kneeling boy shudder. I worked my hands down his chest and felt every new muscle he worked so hard to develop. For me. When I reached his belly and aimed for his groin, Zayn spread a smattering of herbs on #99's forehead.

I felt him tremble. Then I heard it loud and clear. He groaned his slave song to me.

We stayed like that while he sang. Zayn was pouring reassurance into the boy while I drenched him with my ownership. A boy's first taste of my single-tail is life-altering. I wanted #99 to feel safe — protected — when he suffered my whip's kiss.

The reason I had Zayn prepare him was important. A former POW who was tortured needed all the mettle he could muster to trust that he would come to no harm when he was in my hands. Or at the business end of my whip.

I wanted this boy. I had an empty attic cell ready for my next exclusive. With My Cop working remotely at times and Zayn's Tantric talents that sent me into my personal stratosphere, I had use for an in-house exclusive who responded to pain with a purpose. My purpose.

Zayn was there to guide him to that place.

I was going to stripe him. Everywhere.

I had #99 stand up and face me. Zayn nestled behind him and laid his chest on #99's strong back. He gasped when he felt it. That's when something amazing happened.

#99 nodded. He was ready. He knew I would shield him from harm.

I locked his wrists to the overhead bar so he hung in the middle of the room. I could swing from every angle and kiss him with my whip wherever I wanted. I appreciated his history but I don't hold back. Not with my exclusives. Not with him.

Either he would respond the way I wanted or he would shriek in fear. The latter would get him a trip back to the stable dorm and eventually, I'd sell him.

Zayn's eyes were focused on the dangling body, his ears waiting to hear the song. Which melody would he sing? The song of terror from long ago? Or would he sing his slave song to me?

I took two practice swings. Each crack of my whip made #99 tense but his eyes were clear and he never stopped looking at me. He never wavered.

The first stroke left a lovely red welt on his right thigh. The second decorated his left. Zayn felt #99's balls and stepped back, his way of telling me that what he felt was just fine.

Two strokes drew matching stripes on each of his asscheeks. When I rubbed them, he started to sing. He sang louder with each stroke to the back of his legs, between his massive shoulders and inside his thighs.

Zayn was behind him and I felt his brand. He was perfectly balanced and singing his slave song to me. When he gave #99 some of his calm energy, Zayn absorbed all the remnants of fear #99 had left. When #99 sang, Zayn endured each stroke of my whip.

The old man explained it to me months ago. I own Zayn but I share a tiny piece of him with every slave I have him work with. He can't help but take the slave's fear or pain into himself and later, he lets it float away. During that interval, the old man warned, Zayn must be near me so I can feed him a little of his aura to stay balanced.

I wish I understood it more but watching it happen between him and #99 showed me everything I needed to know.

My whip met #99 over and over. Each time, Zayn winced a little but never stopped grunting out his song. When I was finished, I listened to the duet. Zayn stopped.

#99 was singing a solo.

I let him down from the beam and he collapsed on the carpet. Zayn touched his shoulder and mine. That's when I understood.

My slave was pouring his devotion into me through Zayn. I didn't feel any of his fear, that was finally gone. #99 was perfectly calm.

I felt unbelievably powerful.

-=o=-

I let #99 rest while Zayn directed the fire inside me to levels higher than the attic roof. He felt me demand a third time but before he chose the herbs and oils, I saw him look away. Down. At the body panting on the floor. He grabbed him with one hand and pulled #99 closer to me.

Zayn drew a circle of oil around #99's lips and angled his head toward me. I've had exclusives tantalize my breasts before but this time was unparalleled. It wasn't how hard #99 licked and sucked. It was an unreal experience. The fire rekindled and burned through me. No other part of me was touched, just his lips on my breasts.

I knew it, Zayn felt it and #99 completed the circle.

My fingers traced Zayn's brand and my other hand found the small bit of testicle sac under #99's cock cage that wasn't covered. While they sang, I added two items on my agenda.

I was going to put #99 in the attic. And I was going to brand him. Having three exclusives isn't too many. It's the perfect number.

Then I would give him a name.

CHAPTER 25

Au Revoir

THREE WEEKS LATER, it was time for Danica to leave my world and take ownership of her own. Her slave's plane would land in an hour, drop off Mason, and then fly her and her boy to Destiny. The construction was done. Mason uploaded video to show me the results and he said in the voiceover that it was very attractive and functional but not as beautiful as Amityworld.

Damned right.

Danica and I sat on the terrace overlooking the grounds. The stable ran down one slaveway and up another as they went about their daily tasks. When it was time for the second exercise session, I had Jack line them up them outside. Watching that many physically fit male slaves grunting through pushups, weight lifting, squats and run-falls was our entertainment. Their sweat glistened in the warm sun under a cloudless sky.

Danica had a lot to say. "I can't believe how much I've gotten done in three weeks! I owe it all to you, Ms. Amity."

No, she didn't owe me anything. If Danica didn't have the makings of a great Domme, I wouldn't have been invited her back.

"I can hardly wait to have the pilot circle Destiny so I can see it from the sky. I know it will be beautiful."

Yes, it would. Just not *quite* as beautiful as Amityworld.

"Remember what I told you. You have an Intake process, all the tools you need and a slave who will pluck every hair out of their bodies. Keep them hairless or find your own way to even them out. Reduce them to sameness."

"I remember everything you said. Especially about exclusives."

Buying an exclusive or upgrading a slave to that level isn't done lightly. We talked for hours about exclusives and how to use them.

"My boy, I *thought* he was my exclusive. I mean, he was my first slave. And look at everything he's given me! But I was wrong and you were right."

Late one night, I sent Aussie to fetch her boy and bring him to us. He was a proper slave, eager for his daily whipping. I turned him into a relentless worker. But he wasn't exclusive material. I was going to make Danica see that.

#99 was at my feet, waiting for an instruction. It was only his third week living in the attic so he still had a lot to learn. But his entire being hungered to serve me. That wasn't the case with #55.

Her boy craved her ownership. He looked forward to the pain she inflicted because he knew it had a purpose. What he failed at was the basic definition of an exclusive. A boy who satisfies my personal needs. My sensual needs.

The best Dommes overflow with those needs.

Her boy was a slave, a very good one, an excellent one but didn't have the essential innate sense that felt where her sensuality came from. He would never give her a night filled with orgasms. Hell, the orgasm he gave her at breakfast weeks ago was purely amateur. He belonged in the stable, treated the same as every other boy she owned.

It took only four orgasms from Zayn for Danica to realize what her boy lacked. At least she didn't offer to buy Zayn, as much as she wanted him. If she tried, she'd have to fly commercial when I threw her out.

No one touches my exclusives except me.

The slaves were counting their never-ending reps in a loud cadence. Otherwise, it was silent on the terrace.

"Let's get you and your boy to the airport," I said. I held her hands and said, "Anything. Any time. Just call."

"I know I can and I will. Calling you my friend is the best gift I've ever gotten."

I laughed. "Second to Destiny."

We bid each other au revoir and I promised to take her up on her invitation to visit Destiny. There was one last piece of business.

"What name did you give him?" I asked.

"I call him Jonah," she said. "You know, he needed me to rescue him from his own beasts and demons."

It was an apt name for her boy. Even if it had two syllables.

"And yours?" Danica asked.

"I call him Gage." What I didn't tell her was that it means 'oath' or 'pledge' and implies commitment, determination and strong character.

Not to mention his 8.5-inch cock. Soft.

Epilogue

AMITYWORLD WAS QUIET when Danica and her newly-named boy, Jonah, left. I had spent so much time with her, there was a list of tasks I had to take care of. Nova kept a lid on things but she can't — nor is she allowed to — solve problems or go near slave issues. Like the one I had to take care of with some of my females.

Zayn spent every day with Gage, my former #99. I assigned him to make sure Gage was on an even keel and submitting to his role properly as my third exclusive. I summoned Zayn every night for a report and was pleased to hear that Gage had moved beyond his painful history, although pieces of it would always be a part of him. Gage was in the here and now, Zayn felt. In fact, he said Gage had come close but hadn't yet touched his own nirvana. He was capable of it, but Zayn couldn't make it happen for him.

Of course not. When Gage first touched his Tantric heaven, it would be when I wanted him to. And where. And with me.

After taking care of many of the issues I put on hold while Danica was here, I was ready for some fun. My kind of fun. That often involves one of my single-tails. But not today. I had bigger plans.

I was feeding Gage blueberries under the table at breakfast. Aussie was licking his bowl in the corner. The first decision I had to make was one I put off making for weeks. Today was the day.

"Aussie, fetch my chefs."

They trotted into the small dining room behind my dog. He raised his head to hand me the leash in his teeth. Both chefs wore little frilly pink aprons, their kitchen outfits. I put my hand out and they untied the aprons and handed them to me. Aside from their cock cages, they were naked. It was easy for me to see where they added the right kind of bulk when I had them pirouette. On their toes.

"Aussie, bring me the one whose food tastes better."

The poor dog was in a conundrum. Aussie ate everything he was given and licked his bowl clean. Every time. He whined.

"That's the problem, boys," I said to the chefs. "Every meal has been delicious. I'm keeping you both."

The chefs landed on their knees in relief. But it was short lived.

"The first screwup, the first tasteless dish, the first incorrect wine choice — that one is getting sold. Don't let it be you."

I could see gears spinning in their heads, planning menus and choosing wine. Every slave should enjoy a few compliments. Only for a moment.

"Aussie, take them back to the kitchen!"

The dog ran behind the kneeling cooks and nipped at their asses until they ran out of sight. I was certain my upcoming meals would be delightful.

"You! Up!" I grabbed Gage's cage and dragged him to his knees next to my chair. "Show me your ass!"

The boy twisted and laid his hands out as far as he could reach. He parted his knees when I put my hand on his cheek. I jolted Nova to fetch an injector and with no fanfare, plunged it deep inside him and pressed the button. Seconds later, he was flat on the floor.

A drop of purple gel will do that to a slave. Even a highly decorated military officer.

I walked in front of him so all his eyes could see were my stilettos. They were purple, the same color as the gel that invaded his body and obliterated his ability to think. That's the beauty of the purple gel. The old man concocted it to make any slave highly suggestible. What I say is the only thing he can hear. He is rendered absolutely obedient. Unquestioning. Beyond compliant.

"You will stay at my feet today. You will not think about anything else. You will never be more than 12 inches away from me at any time. When I run you across the grounds, you will follow every instruction I issue."

He would stay on his belly until his arms and legs started working again, a second effect of the gel. While I enjoyed my breakfast and my second cup of coffee, he began slithering toward my ankle. When I visited the kitchen to review the upcoming food order, Gage scurried to be behind me. No matter where I went, he fought to be near me, especially when Aussie growled at him for horning in on his place. I had a latte delivered to the terrace and used the stairs this time. Gage crawled up the staircase behind me, lumbering on each step. When I sat on a lounge chair, Gage tried to wrap himself around my feet. That's when Aussie bit his ass. He yelped, Aussie nosed him aside and Nova appeared.

Nova is the only female I kept out of regular fitness exercises. She has a special program that increases her stamina but doesn't diminish her bulk. I enjoy watching her huge breasts and layers of fat wiggle and waggle when she runs. She could run across the grounds now without gasping for air. Well, not gasping too hard.

After granting her permission to speak, she said, "Your females are in position."

I was golf-carted to the punishment building with Gage running furiously behind, fighting to stay as close as possible to the cart's rear bumper. Good thing his fitness program was recently upgraded or he'd have been dragged behind by the chain clamped to his ring.

He never looked to his left or right. As far as Gage was concerned, the only thing in his field of vision was me.

CHAPTER 26

Punishing Females

I KEEP ONLY ENOUGH females to take care of the main house, a few who also do double-duty in Intake and Medical and Jack and her girls in the stable dorm. Then there's Nova. Some days, I have trouble counting her as a female. Today's tally showed an even dozen of them.

My house manager, a 45-ish year-old female I've had for three years, rates the females' work every day. Those ratings go to Nova who enters them into the database and I glance at the reports before dinner. Danica's visit interrupted my schedule. When I finally got to the reports, I didn't like what I saw.

I was looking at a distinct downward trend.

There are two solutions to deal with females who slack off. One is to punish them. The other is to sell them. Of course, there's always a third lurking in their future. Expulsion.

I do not believe in punishing individual females who are part of a set. They have to work together seamlessly or not at all. Four years ago, I sold six females on the same day. The remainder learned their lesson quickly, especially when they found out where they wound up. I didn't care about the new owner's revolting reputation, although the leftover girls certainly did. I almost never have to deal with problems with my females. Until today.

When I arrived at the punishment building with Gage dripping sweat but no farther than arm's length behind me, the females were strapped to a long table, ankles and wrists locked with spreader bars between their legs. Their position was intended to fill them with fear and it always delivers. I added an extra touch today and covered their heads. I didn't care which was which. As far as I was concerned, they were all guilty.

Group punishment is superior to making an example of one or two. At least it is with females. That's why all my slaves, including females, are chipped.

Gage was on his knees at my side but knew this was not a time to snuggle around my feet. Even on his knees, he carried the proud air of a military officer. His pride in my ownership? It's one of many reasons he was about to become permanent.

The females are used to having their perineal chips jolted. Those shocks are quick and I usually set them to low. That's enough to tell them they've been summoned.

Not today. I set the level to medium and twisted the dial to "all."

The screaming started the second I pressed the button. Loud wails and gut-level screeches filled the building. I rubbed Gage's bald head and felt him relax with my touch. I'm sure he heard too much shrieking when he was held captive and some of them might well have been his own. While the chips did their work, I kept my palm on his scalp to make sure no hideous memories invaded his thoughts.

What I felt was the purple gel working perfectly. I don't think Gage actually heard the girls. He was totally focused on staying next to my right leg and my hand on his bald head.

Twenty seconds later, I turned them off. The noise faded and was replaced by female sobbing. Weeping women don't affect me. I own them. They are *not* my friends. They are lucky I feed and house them. They knew the other option might well be the Domme, the gal whose nickname in my network is Cruella, that I sold six of them to a while ago.

I turned the level to high.

This time they bellowed from pure pain. They couldn't see anything with bags covering their heads. They couldn't predict what I would do to them next. I let that pain and the fear of more fill their bodies.

Thirty seconds later, I let them breathe while I decided if they learned their lesson. I had Nova unbag the house manager to answer for all of them.

"Tell me why you are being punished."

She could barely speak. Her voice was raspy from screaming and her face was stained with tears, drool and clumps of snot.

"I am responsible for their unsatisfactory performance."

That was true but if she thought I would release the others and punish only her, she was wrong. There are no martyrs in my household.

"And?" I said. It wasn't really a question and she knew it.

She tried to pull herself together to reply but was having trouble figuring out what to say. Her first try was dismal. "Their work was unacceptable."

I jolted them all again. High.

She shouted, "OUR WORK WAS UNACCEPTABLE!"

She got it right that time.

I had Nova unbag the rest of them and issued the only ultimatum they would ever hear from me.

"I have a buyer overseas looking for twelve trained females to service his vile bordello. One mistake by any of you and the entire lot will be shipped across the ocean. Do I make myself clear?"

To a female, they bounced their asses on the table in a resounding chorus of yeses.

"Get them back to work," I told Nova. She led them as they ran in a straight line across the fields to the slave door. I expected to see a sparkling main house when I was done here.

Dealing with slave disobedience is tedious but necessary. Before I had Gage run behind my cart back to the main house, I looked around the training building's main room.

Over in the far corner, I saw one of the new punishment benches isolated from the others. Behind it was a portable heater. A metal pole stood next to it. On one end was a big "A".

CHAPTER 27

MY COP

WHEN MY COP was unpacked in the transport garage, I felt a wave of relief surge through the main house. My females were working tirelessly day and night the past weeks and the house was definitely in ship-shape. Sometimes you have to remind your property what the consequences are for slacking off. I find it more effective to show them. They knew better than to rub their still-aching crotches. Long-lasting correction is only type I use. I don't have time or interest to oversee those details so I let their pussies do the talking. Or screaming.

My Cop had been in-country on assignment for too many weeks. That's all I know or want to know about what he does when he works remotely. The only thing that matters is what he does when he returns to me. If you have a remote slave like My Cop, you understand.

I'm the only Domme I know who has a slave like My Cop.

Zayn and Gage tried to keep me satisfied during those busy weeks but my sensual desires were all over the map. Zayn intuited it one night when I sent for him. He didn't ask for permission to speak; rather, he let his herbs do the talking. It was a lovely night but not overly memorable. Before I sent him back to his attic cell, he rested his forehead on mine and spread his fingers on my temples.

"He is safe. Now."

Damn. I can't keep secrets from a Tantric guide with Zayn's skills who can literally *feel* what I'm worried about. Even Gage was concerned when I didn't summon him three nights in a row. That's why I injected him with the purple gel, to make him understand I will use him when I care to. If I have no need for him, his job is to stay close and wait until I do.

I was in my office when Nova wriggled through the slave door, squatted at my feet and waited for my nod. She's gotten better at long-term squatting and can run longer distances without gasping too hard for air. My slave trainer took my promise very seriously that I would cut off one of his testicles if she didn't improve in two weeks.

"He pleads for your time," she said.

I knew who *he* was. I was concerned about what his last assignment did to him. It's unusual for him to be gone that long without contacting me via our private system. Not hearing from him meant one thing. Something was wrong, something had happened, something I didn't want to know had taken place.

Damnit, I wanted to know every detail.

"Aussie, fetch My Cop."

The dog crawled to the slave door and this time, had to twist his huge front shoulders to fit through it. The slave trainer I bought was doing a competent job. At least I didn't have to deal with that issue.

It took ten long minutes for Aussie to bark for permission to enter. I jolted his chip. That's every slave's cue to drop whatever they're doing, no matter where they are, and report to me. The dog squirmed his way through the opening and a few steps behind him was My Cop.

From across the room, he looked like My Cop. Something was different. I could feel it.

As he crept toward me, I counted the scars, the bruises, the staples that closed gashes and the black-and-purple abrasions on his arms and back. I felt sick. No one gets to hurt My Cop. Except me.

Someone broke my rule. Pain must *always* have *my* purpose.

Aussie sensed how upset I was and hid in a corner. My Cop — or what was left of his battered body — knelt at my feet. He tried to extend his arms and drop his forehead to the floor but the groan he let out wasn't even close to his slave song.

It was a cacophony of agony.

I was nauseated. More than that, I was damned furious at whoever did this to him.

I rolled my chair toward him and held his head in my lap. His face was hot and his skin burned wherever I touched. He mumbled "Ms. Amity owns me," over and over.

"Tell me," I said.

I knew he couldn't divulge all the details about what he'd been through. I told myself I didn't *want* to know. It didn't work. This time, I *had* to know.

It took a long time for My Cop to explain what he could share. He couldn't form sentences, just horrific phrases. I never let go of his head while he tried to talk. A complicated mission. Hostages rescued. His team ambushed. Weeks of torture. Taking out the kidnappers. Crawling through the jungle. An R&R copter rescue.

He ended with this.

"The only thing that got me through it, the only thing I had to hold onto, was what was in my gut. 'Ms. Amity owns me, Ms. Amity owns me …' I had to get back here. To you. It's where I want to be … where I *have* to be … if I couldn't get back to you, I didn't want to be anywhere … I didn't want to live anymore."

My hands hurt from hugging his head so hard. There was no way on this green earth that I would let go.

When he's working remotely, I unlock My Cop's cock cage. Nova puts it in the silver box I keep in my sight until he returns. That box was sitting on my desk, waiting for me to unlock it and put its contents where it belonged.

He didn't *want* the cage. He was alive because he *needed* it.

"Please, please Ms. Amity, keep me. Don't get rid of me. I know … I'm so sorry. I look like hell … I'm not good enough for you anymore."

He didn't look like hell. Not to me. He looked perfect.

I sent a message to Nova to gather the female staff and the chefs. I issued their new instructions.

"Set up a hospital bed in my suite. Make my grandmother's chicken soup according to her recipe."

"Aussie! Fetch Emma!"

-=o=-

Amityworld went on autopilot for the weeks it took My Cop to heal. Emma saw him at least three times every day and handled the IV and antibiotics to prevent infection like the pro she is. Emma dressed demurely. This wasn't a time for pink frills.

I worked out of my rooms and kept an eye on his recovery. He slept a lot and mumbled in his dreams. "Ms. Amity owns me … Ms. Amity owns me ..." Each time he woke up, the first thing he did was search the suite to find me. For those weeks, I was there every time he looked.

I brought in a trauma specialist from the city, a former military physician who still had security clearance. He agreed to my conditions for anonymity.

"Haven't seen anything like this since Iraq," he said. "Amazing that nothing critical is broken, well not completely. The bastards knew what they were doing."

He was right about one thing. They were bastards.

Emma recommended getting My Cop a physical therapist so I contacted Ned with my order. The next morning, I inspected one on video and bought him. Red Rick, who owed My Cop two favors for his help with a sticky situation in Memphis and one involving a poorly timed flat tire on his delivery truck and overly-helpful state troopers, had the slave in my transport garage six hours later. I have the best friends.

There are some secrets that are hard to keep in my network. I was inundated with calls from my friends who knew something happened to one of my slaves and were hoping it wasn't My Cop. They didn't learn much from the gossip. But I did.

We care about each other. I adore my Domme friends.

A week later on a Thursday afternoon, My Cop woke up and asked to speak to me.

"Please, Ms. Amity, own me."

"I will *always* own you," I said. It was what he needed to hear and easy for me to say because it was the simple truth. I sat next to his bed, reached under the sheet and held his uncaged cock in my hand. "I will *never* let go of you."

For only the second time since he gave himself to me, My Cop really cried. Sobbed. For the first time, so did I.

He was mending well. At least his body was. No one survives torture like that without scars. Bodies heal. Minds take longer.

Doctors, a trauma specialist, a physical therapist all had a place in My Cop's recovery. But the other part, his tortured thoughts, were mine alone to repair.

I sent for the ancient Asian Master and explained what I wanted to do, to heal the nightmares of torture. The old man has an awareness and perception of all sorts of situations so I hoped he had one to help

My Cop. He arrived the same day I contacted him, concern written all over his face. I listened to his insights.

He held my hands and said, "Big trouble. Unspeakable pain. Silent mystery. Survival."

Damnit, the old man did it again.

We stood in my office, his fingers intertwined with mine as he absorbed my outrage — my fury — at the barbarity those bastards did to My Cop. He thought for a few minutes and said, "Get the boy. We need a dark place to work."

The boy was Zayn. He showed up in minutes after I jolted him. The place was the butler's pantry off the kitchen. Running water, no windows and plenty of flat space to mix oils and herbs.

"One more," the old man said. "The other boy. The one who knows this atrocity."

How the hell did the old man know about Gage?

A jolt later, Gage ran in and the three of them were closeted in the butler pantry. I had no doubt the old man knew what the 'big trouble' was and who suffered unspeakable pain. Sometimes it's better not to try to understand how he figures things out and just go with it. This was the definition of one of those times.

My females tiptoed around the kitchen, staying as far away from me as possible while I paced outside the pantry door. The chefs asked if they could prepare something for me to eat. Once. One look told them I wasn't hungry. Not for food.

My Cop was broken. A different kind of hunger filled me. I wanted him whole. I wanted to kill the bastards who dared damage My Cop.

A long time later, the door opened. Zayn came out first, followed by Gage. From the looks on their faces, I knew something important, something very demanding on them had taken place behind the closed door. The last to emerge was the old man. He held a tiny bottle in his fingers. It was white.

"Take me to him," he said. "I need these two with me."

I've learned not to question what old man asks for. If he could help My Cop, anything he wanted was his. We rode upstairs in the elevator in silence. When we arrived at the door to my suite's foyer, he stepped in front of me. He was going inside and I wasn't.

"I will call for you when it is time," he said.

Zayn stood on my right and Gage on my left. I held their cages in my fists. When he's with the old man, Zayn is always balanced so I didn't bother tracing my brand to check. We waited without speaking because there was nothing to say.

I don't know how long we stood there but when the door opened, I was ready to march in. The old man asked me to let go of Zayn and Gage and pointed at them to follow him inside. He closed the damned door again. I tried one more time not to be angry and failed. Again. But I stood there, waiting impatiently, until he needed me.

A deafening groan filled my ears. It pierced the door and echoed throughout the hallway. I know my exclusives' songs and this definitely was not one of them. It was forceful. Like a trumpet blast. Then I heard a gut-wrenching scream. My gut. My Cop's scream.

Was the old man torturing My Cop?

It was all I could do to trust him. And Zayn. And hope I made the right decision about Gage. For the first time I could remember when I didn't have a whip in my hand, my palms were damp.

The door finally opened. The old man said, "He needs you."

I followed him inside. The scene that greeted me was powerful. Overpowering. Zayn was kneeling on one side of the bed, Gage on the other. Their elbows were locked with My Cop's arms and all three had their eyes closed. The boys on their knees were concentrating so hard they didn't notice — or care — that I was there. My Cop was close to hyperventilating. The tension in the room was tangible. I could feel the intensity dripping out of Gage. Zayn was sucking in air and blowing it out rapidly. My Cop was rigid. Every muscle in his body was tense.

The old man was smiling. He had to be feeling the anger that was pouring out of me.

"Ms. Amity, own your slave."

He didn't have to say it twice. I walked to the bed, reached under the covers and held his naked cock with both of my hands. In seconds, several things happened.

Zayn's breathing slowed.

Gage's eyes opened.

My Cop's entire body relaxed.

I felt ultimate power swirl inside me.

-=o=-

Over oolong tea and blueberry scones in my suite, the old man explained what happened. He used Zayn to soak up My Cop's agony. It wasn't physical pain. It was his terror that he was no longer good enough for me. Gage shared his strength at moving past his own torture with My Cop who always thought of himself as the rescuer, not the one who needed saving. Both of them worked until they were exhausted, the way the old man warned them they had to if the new potion in the white bottle was going to work.

"This man, your most special one, judged himself to be a disappointment to you, even though he withstood torture, never gave information to the enemy. Believing himself to be a failure, he thought you no longer would want him."

That's stupid, I thought.

"It is *not* stupid," the old man said.

I've given up trying to figure out how he knows what I'm thinking.

"It was your ownership that made him survive. Being your property — the only thing he has ever wanted — was the force that gave him strength. Your other two were near collapse, taking on themselves his fear of your rejection and giving him their strength. He needed you — they all needed you to complete the circle."

"What did the white potion do?" I asked.

"Ah, Ms. Amity, that did nothing. Nothing at all. It was their belief in its curative power that made it work."

Damn, the old man mind-fucked my exclusives! I thought that was my job. But it worked, so I chose to go with it.

I offered him payment and he refused. "It is my honor to help you and three males who are the most important to you."

Before he left, I made sure Nova tucked several hundred-dollar bills into his kit. The old man had one more request, one more inexplicable example of his connection to my thoughts.

"May I be privileged to watch you brand your new exclusive?"

CHAPTER 28

THE SIZZLING A

BRANDING AN EXCLUSIVE is not something I do lightly. Or often. Only the very few I choose, the ones who give themselves to me completely and utterly, are allowed to wear my brand on the underside of their testicles. To be one of my exclusives and wear my brand, a slave must accept that his only mission for the rest of his life is to satisfy me. Intimately. Whenever I want.

It's a lifelong bond. An exclusive has to covet it as much as he values his own life. In return, he enjoys my ownership and know I will keep him safe for as long as I want him. They work to make me want them all day. Every day. And night.

They are never typical slaves. Even though I call them special, that word doesn't come close to defining them. I can sense that amorphous quality. I felt it in Gage when My Cop first asked me to meet him. But Gage, then a nameless male I took in for two days as a small trinket I gifted My Cop, burned with that spark. The problem was that his history, his time as a POW and the torture he suffered, blocked his ability to understand what his life's goal really was.

He wanted — he yearned — to be owned, to be safe, to please his owner. What I did during those two days was force him to reach deep inside, beneath the awful memories, and destroy the roadblocks he built to survive captivity. Once he did, and it took a lot of work, he finally understood what he was meant to be.

Not a slave. *My* slave.

I monitored him for two years and watched his progress. He finally retired from the military and begged for an audience with me. Two weeks later, he was delivered to my transport garage and I sent him through Intake.

He was hardly a one-trick slave. Gage had four talents. He used all of them last night when I had him in my rooms until dawn. It isn't easy to describe what his fingers can do. No herbs, no oils. Just his fingers and his inborn understanding of how, where and when to use them.

Today was his branding day.

Ordinarily, I don't allow anyone to watch a branding. But this one was, just like the slave, special. The old man had earned an invitation.

I wanted Zayn there. My connection with him would grow when a third exclusive was put in an attic cell near his. Attending the branding would enhance our silent way of communicating. And my nights would be much better.

My Cop, who was released from 24-hour bedrest and was progressing beyond the physical therapist's predictions, was the other. He was grateful for what he called my saving a good man's life. I explained that Gage was a *very* good man and an even better slave who would make an exceptional exclusive. But he — My Cop — was different.

He was a lot more than simply special.

For the first time since he crept into my office battered and bruised, he could kneel at my feet without groaning in pain. "Ms. Amity owns me," he said in a clear, firm voice.

My Cop was back. It was time to brand Gage.

-=o=-

Jack and Nova took care of the preparations. The iron was red hot and the building's cameras were off. One new bench was ready for its cargo.

The old man and I rode in the cart across the grounds. My Cop and Zayn knelt in the back. Gage ran behind us, his head held high and his legs churning like an elk in the forest. He was where he belonged. He didn't know where he was going and what was going to happen there. Slaves never need to know my agenda. They accept whatever I demand without question, just like Gage was doing now.

Gage was beautiful when he ran.

The onlookers took their places on the floor behind the bench. Gage glanced at them and then at the punishment bench and knew where he belonged. The aroma from the sizzling branding iron filled everyone's nostrils. Gage trembled. Briefly.

Gage squared his shoulders and marched to the bench. Not a tremor, not a shudder. He was resolute in his belief that I would protect him, that he was safe when he was with me. That lesson would be seared into his mind — and his balls — very soon.

No one locks down my exclusives except me. The injector held one drop of black gel. I slipped it deep into him and pressed the button. The black gel is perfect. White is emptiness; the absence of color. Black is the presence of all shades and hues. Ten seconds later, it hit him.

Black potion fills a slave's mind with uncontrollable need. It defeats their fears and conquers their bodily control. Their minds empty. The old man explained that it smashes the last ounce of any rational thinking. To Gage, there was no one in the building but me. The one — the only — presence he could perceive was mine.

The secret is that black gel can amplify only what is already inside a slave. His submission. To me. All Gage knew, all he could think about was his owner. It saturated inside him like a flood.

"Stop breathing," I said.

Gage held his breath until I gave him permission to breathe. Perfect.

"Bark," I said. Gage yelped like a new puppy.

"You were desperate to be owned and could not admit it to yourself. You confessed it to me. I watched you for two years climb from the bottom of hell to the top of the mountain. You reached the summit. It's the place I call Amityworld. I chose to own you and I will. Forever."

"Beg," I said.

Desperate to obey, Gage pleaded to be branded with the sizzling iron in my hand.

That's exactly what I did.

His screams echoed off the walls and oozed into my other exclusives' ears.

"Who are you?" I asked.

Three slaves roared out the answer. It came from deep inside their guts.

"MS. AMITY OWNS ME!"

The old man smiled.

CHAPTER 29

EXCLUSIVE HUNGER

I KEPT MY NEW EXCLUSIVE in arm's reach the rest of the day. The old man offered herbal tea for the pain that even the black gel couldn't block hours later. Dinner that night was atypical because it had been an exceptional day. It was the celebration of my new exclusive, my three pack. They sat in chairs around the table. Gage winced every time he shifted, something he did frequently that night. Herbal tea only goes so far.

Zayn was unusually talkative after he was told, much to his surprise, that they were all permitted to speak freely. He almost never talks about the old man except to request I send for him, usually after one of Zayn's difficult sessions. Tonight was different. Zayn couldn't say enough about the old man and how much he appreciated his guidance.

I asked Zayn what the ultimate skill the old man could show him would be.

His eyes stared at the chandelier and then at me. "If it is possible, I want to learn how to please you more each day."

I don't know if even an ancient Asian Tantric Master had that many herbs. But I was definitely going to find out.

Gage picked at his food. His focus was obviously on his new brand. Emma tended to it with ointment and an unusually close-up inspection. On all fours. The new cages left room for me to see and feel a slave's brand so his permanent cage was going on after dinner. All I needed was whipped cream to create an unforgettable dessert.

My Cop ate a thick steak done medium rare, his favorite, like a starving man. The specialist and Emma agreed that he was well enough to eat meat and he tore into it with unabashed fervor. It was too soon to feed him his preferred dessert, my whip's kiss, even though I knew he longed for it. Later tonight when I had all three exclusives in my suite, I'd feed him what he needed.

Amityworld felt right. Balanced. I felt a powerful surge of need swirling in my toes. Zayn sensed it and asked if I would allow him to satisfy me tonight.

"It's on my agenda," I said. He grinned. My Cop looked at me with hope in his eyes. Gage put his fork down and stared at his plate.

"Both of you too," I said. "You think your day has been extraordinary? Your night will be exceptional. So will mine."

Aussie poked his snout on my leg and I took the paper out of his teeth. After I read it, I told my exclusives we were taking a trip. To Montana. Danica wanted to host me for a long weekend and asked me to please bring my exclusives.

"You too, Aussie," I said.

My pet dog barked.

"Finish eating," I told my trio. "I'm hungry. Starving. You *all* are going to feed me."

Disclaimer

This is a work of fiction. Any semblance between original characters and real persons, living or dead, is coincidental. The author in no way represents the companies, corporations, or brands mentioned in this book. The likeness of historical/famous figures have been used fictitiously; the author does not speak for or represent these people. All opinions expressed in this book are the author's, or fictional.

About Amity Harris

AMITY HARRIS is one of the most popular Femdom authors online and in print. Her explicit stories bring Female Domination to a new level of intensity readers feel when they read Amity's novels.

She is the author of the original *Debbie's Gift*, an online Femdom classic completely revised and now available in electronic format, and her new novels, *Erection on Demand*, a Femdom medical thriller, *Femdom Slave Training for Delivery*, *The Slave Circus*, *The Swedish Slave Auction*, *The Dominas' Bedtime Stories*, *Maison Brielle*, and *The Training Farm*. She has ten volumes of short stories and novellas available as eBooks at Amazon.

Amity writes about the authentic Femdom life she lives. She has a taste for remote slaves who have skills she can use in her businesses and for her personal pleasure. She keeps exclusive slaves whose lifelong task is to satisfy her. They never know when one of her moods will appear. She keeps them in attic cells so they're close at hand to quench her powerful needs. Whenever. Wherever.

She has provided free online Femdom stories for her fans for years at Amityworld.com. Amityworld is a free members-only website with brand new stories and pictures.

Amity Harris is a lifestyle Femdom and maintains both in-person and remote stables of male and female submissives that she trains and uses. She has a network of like-minded friends who gather at auctions, circuses and parlors to compare notes, share training skills and enjoy each other's company. She has loaned some of her stable to friends and rents to select private clients to live out their secret fetishes and kinks. Everyone compliments her perfectly trained slaves abilities and flawless performances.

Amity's favorite flower is the sunflower, her favorite color is cobalt blue and her biggest vice is top-quality chocolate chip ice cream.

Find out when new stories are online and new novels are published at Amityworld.com.

Books by Amity Harris

Amity Harris's Femdom novels and stories are available in print or electronic format at Amazon: amzn.to/3vkwY39 or use this QR code.

Amity's Femdom Novels
A Weekend in Amityworld (2025)
Keyboard Control (2025)
Destiny – A Lesson in Building a Stable
Reckoning – Turning Men into Merchandise (2024)
Shopping for Rentables (2024)
Sold! To the Highest Bidder (2024)
Debbie's Gift (Electronic 2024)
Erection on Demand (2024)
Femdom Slave Training for Delivery (2023)
Femdom Pet Shoppe (2023)
Slave Training for Delivery
The Swedish Slave Auction (2023)
Amity's Femdom Parlors (2023)
The Slave Circus (2022)
The Dominas' Bedtime Stories, (2022)
Maison Brielle, Grandmother's Femdom Diary (2022)
The Want Ad, Part II, At the Company (2022)
The Want Ad (2020)
The Training Farm, A Journey into Submission (2015)
Ten Short Story Collections, (2016)
Debbie's Gift (Print 2005)

Printed in Great Britain
by Amazon